Secret in the

PEW

PEW

Regina Howard

Published by "A Sound Voice Publishing"
3965-F Cascade Road SW #1136
Atlanta, GA 30331
www.asoundvoicelive.com

Printed in the United States of America

ISBN-13: 978-1477625644
ISBN-10: 147762564X

<u>DEDICATION</u>

I dedicate this book to God, my husband, my daughter, my mother (Mildred Lloyd), my forever friends Traycee and Priscilla (over 30 years of friendship), Sara and Ella for encouraging me to "get er' done" (I love you ladies to life and I am grateful to God for your friendship and sisterhood) and all of the men/women out there, that may have at one time had difficulty staying focused on the plan of God for your life. Know that God is always there for you and you will never have to settle for less. Thank you, to my Pastor Bishop Dale. C. Bronner and my First Lady Dr. Nina D. Bronner for their prayers and continued support (they rock!!!).

PREFACE

This book is designed to encourage and motivate that single or married woman out there that has had a hard time, letting go of the one thing/person that has held you back from being all God has called you to be. Don't let the distractions of life cause your destiny to be delayed. You have the power to walk through the storm and the rain if you will just keep your eyes on God.

I know you have a friend that you see falling off of the beaten path, go after her and help her regain her focus. Let her know, she is not alone. We are all in this together and yes we are our sister's keeper. Take one day at a time and work through any issues you may have. Please, however, don't be the sister with a

"*Secret* in the PEW."

CHAPTER ONE

As I lay here on the bed in the emergency room in an Atlanta, GA hospital, the tears begin to roll down my face. I start to think back on Pastor Gresham's last message. I clearly heard him saying "Be sure your sins will find you out", and "Woe unto to them that know to do and don't". I knew deep down within myself he was speaking to me, the woman with the awesome husband and a "secret in the pew". Now, my sins will find me out, as I try to explain to my husband Kristopher about my car accident and the dead man in the passenger seat.

It all started last year about six months before the wedding. I was leaving a meeting at my job. I had so much on my mind and a lot in my hands. My best friend had just passed away and that was very hard for me considering we had known one another since Kindergarten.

I was leaving the office, not really paying attention and I bumped into the gentleman that conducted our meeting. I dropped everything in my hands and knocked everything out of his. He was so polite about it though. I think I must have said "I'm so sorry" at least fifteen times. He helped me pick up our things, reached out to shake my hand and said "Hi, I'm Kristopher Thompson, but everyone calls me Kris." I smiled and said, "I remember, from your introduction in the meeting. I'm Passion Taylor." He smiled and said "That's a name, I'm sure I won't forget." I must say he was quite handsome, had a gorgeous smile, smelled great and was very well dressed. He wore a tan suite, with an off white French cuffed shirt. His cufflinks were silver and tan and matched his tie clip. He had on some nice brown loafer style shoes that looked brand new. He was what any sister in her right mind dreamed about.

We both walked out to the parking lot sharing small talk, mostly about the meeting. I have walked to that parking lot over one thousand times but I never reached my car so fast. We said "good night," and went our separate ways.

About a week had passed and Kris was at the office to meet with my boss. We passed one another in the hallway and each said "good morning." It was about 9:50am I went to my office, shut the door and prepared quickly for a 10:00am conference call. The call lasted a little over an hour, it ended just in time for lunch. I walked out of my office and right into Kris. "Off to lunch?" He asked. "Yes", I said. He responded with, "Would you like some company?" I was shocked that he would even ask me to go along. He had such a wonderful smile on his face I couldn't refuse him. I didn't have any special plans, so I thought some company would be nice. I asked Kris if he wanted to go to any place in particular, and he said he knew of a fantastic sandwich shop downtown and it was relatively close so we went. We ordered lunch and had a very good conversation. Kris shared with me, how he was once married to a wonderful woman for three years. "She was diagnosed with breast cancer, a year and a half into our marriage," he said. "We met in the singles' ministry at church. We would talk on the phone for hours about life and the word. At first we were not even considering dating but then after much private time in prayer I knew I wanted her to be my wife. There was something so special about her. She was such a calm woman. When I was anxious about anything, she would take me by my hand and begin to pray. I promise every single time she did that it would make things so much better. I still miss her." I sat there in silence, it seemed like I was there for hours. After searching for the right words to say, I finally said "I'm sorry for your loss, it sounds like you really loved her."

Lunch was over, I had to get back to my office and Kris had a meeting to attend some where else. After exchanging our phone numbers and personal email addresses, we said our good byes.

When I got to the office, there was a message on my desk. I read it once, and then I read it twice more. I thought to myself this can't be. The message was from Terry St. James. He's a guy I met in college and dated up until a year ago. What could he want I wondered? The break up wasn't bitter, but it did hurt. We're talking about a seven year relationship. I did something I knew I should never have done. I picked up that phone and dialed Terry's number.

"Hello, this is Terry," was all I heard before freezing up over the sound of that deep sexy voice. I got myself together and said "Hi, Terry its Passion returning your call." "Hey there beautiful, I was thinking about you and thought I'd give you a call." I was about to melt like butter hearing his voice and picturing that brother's body. "That was nice of you Terry, but what is this call really about?" He laughed and said "You still know me, don't you?" Like the back of my hand I thought. "Well I wanted to see you tonight, have dinner and talk." I was not in the mood for any craziness, so I asked what he wanted to talk about. "If I remember correctly Terry, our last conversation started this way and ended with a break up." It was so quiet, you could hear cotton fall on carpet. "Baby listen", he said. "I'm sorry about ending every thing the way I did, but at the time, it seemed like the thing to do. I miss talking to you and spending time with you. Passion, I need you in my life." I wait a moment before speaking, "Terry, over the last past year I have managed to move forward. I am going to church now and active in a couple of ministries." Terry interrupts, "You were going to church when we were dating." Quickly, I responded with "I know you aren't trying to judge me." "No, I'm not", he said "That came out all wrong." "Listen, Terry all I'm saying is, I have moved on I don't want any set backs." He said "Passion, I'm not calling you

10

to play any games, I just want to talk." For some reason I felt like he was telling me the truth. "Okay, we can talk." Almost yelling he says, "Thank you, baby." I cut him off by saying "It can't be tonight though, because I'm going to church. You'll have to wait until tomorrow." "I really wanted….," "Terry," I said sounding aggravated. "Okay, Passion tomorrow night. Does 7:30 at the Lilac Café sound fine?" "Yes, that's fine I'll see you then."

Before I knew it, the day was done. Generating reports and in and out of meetings can totally cause time to fly.

The day is over and I'm off to church. Praise and Worship was awesome. The young lady that leads the Praise and Worship team certainly knows how to usher the people into God's presence. I was somewhat excited about this one night revival. I had heard nothing but good things about the guest preacher, so I was ready to hear the word.

As the preacher was being introduced, I looked around the sanctuary. My eyes must have been playing tricks on me. I saw a man over to my right that looked just like Kris. The speaker took the platform and began to preach his message. I was blown away, by such knowledge of the word as well as his delivery. He said some things that hit me right in my heart. He extended the opportunity, for those of us who wanted to come and rededicate our lives to come to the altar, and I went. More than anyone around me, I knew I really needed to rededicate. I felt so renewed when I left the altar, I wanted to call everyone I knew and share it with them. As I turned to go back to my seat, who came up to hug me with a large smile on his face? You guessed it, Kris. He hugged me and whispered in my ear, "God bless you." I stepped back and said, "Thank you". He was still smiling. "I am so surprised to see you here" he said. "I was surprised to see you as well. Not, like you wouldn't go to church or anything, just plain old fancy meetin' you here." We laughed. Kris motioned for me to go ahead and as I prepared to sit down I noticed Kris was coming to sit beside me. I slid over and he sat with me and walked me to my car after service.

Once we were in the parking lot Kris asked "Would you like to go grab a bite to eat?" It wasn't too late, so I said "sure". We went to a small diner and engaged in conversation about the service. We both agreed that the service was anointed. "Passion tell me a little bit about yourself." I looked at Kris and said "There really isn't much to tell. I'm a member of the church we just left, you know where I work and I am the middle child of three children, two girls and one boy. I love to read, travel and go to the movies. That's about it." "Okay, that was good." Kris said smiling. "You were talking so fast, like you were nervous or something. Are you okay, with coming out to eat?" I replied, "Yes, I'm fine. I just wasn't expecting that question. Not like it was hard or anything." Kris sat back in his seat with that ever so beautiful smile on his face, with a look of approval in his eyes. It was really different. The waitress interrupted by saying,

"Your diet coke mam and your water sir." We both said "Thank you". "Are you ready to order?" Kris looked at me and I nodded yes. "The lady will order first", he said. I found that to be refreshing, considering I had only gone out with groups, girlfriends or by myself here of late. We ordered our meals and continued talking. Kris made a comment about something that happened during the service and we laughed hysterically. Our laughter was calmed down by Kris' cell phone ringing. "Excuse me, I have to take this. Hi Mom, how are you? I'm fine. I'm out with a friend having a bite to eat. What are you up to? Is dad okay? Mom, I'm fine. God has my best interest at heart and I will continue the healing process and come out like a champ." I sat there thinking about how he was so patient with his mom and how she was so concerned about his well being. "Okay, mom, I will. I love you and we'll talk this weekend, see you later."

The waitress came at the perfect time. "Grilled chicken caesar salad for the lady and blackened tilapia for the gentleman. Do you all need anything else?" "No, thank you we're fine." I said.

I was relaxed laughing and talking to Kris. He was such a gentleman and he appeared to be genuine. "So, are you and your parents close?" He looked me in my eyes and said "Yes, we are. Especially since Melanie passed away. My folks knew her death really took a toll on me and they have done everything they could to make sure I was comfortable. Even to the point of saying I could move back home." I was thinking to myself "how sweet."

"That's a blessing", I said. "So many people don't have that type of a relationship with their parents on a regular basis." Kris nodded and said, "You're right. It seems as if family doesn't matter much any more. What about you and your parents? What is your relationship like?" I smiled. "My parents are my heroes. They've been married for forty years and I can only remember my father being nothing but sweet to my mom. That however, didn't stop them from spanking our butts." Kris agreed with a loud laugh.

We stopped talking long enough, to finish our food. I excused myself to the restroom, because I just could not sit there any longer. When I came back to the table, the waitress was walking away. "Did I miss anything?" I said. "No, you didn't, I was taking care of the check," he said.

We walked outside and bid each other good night and he said he would call me sometime during the week. I went home with a song in my heart and a smile on my face. It was good to go out, have fun, enjoy being with a man and it just be cordial. I will never get caught up in another dead end relationship again.

CHAPTER TWO

When I woke up this morning I was still smiling. Last night was somewhat magical. I took my shower, got dressed and left for work. Today was going to be busy as usual, being the Executive Assistant to the vice president of a major publishing company was no piece of cake. My boss however, is an awesome man. Lawrence A. Pittman, husband, father of four, charity worker and the Assistant Pastor of our church. He's a kind man even when it comes to having to discipline an employee. Let me explain. When Peggy Alexander was late everyday for one week straight, Mr. Pittman had me call her and tell her he needed to see her in his office. When she came in for the meeting, I could tell she was nervous. As she sat in my office waiting she was constantly rubbing her hands together. Quietly she said, "I'm about to be fired aren't I?" I was shocked that she even said anything. I looked up from my work, smiled and told her "It will be alright, no matter what just tell the truth." She slightly smiled back. My phone rang, it was Mr. Pittman. I responded to the voice on the other end with a "Yes, sir". Ms. Alexander, Mr. Pittman will see you now." She went into his office and didn't surface for another thirty-five minutes. When she came out of the office, she turned around to Mr. Pittman and said, "Thank you so much for understanding." She looked at me and said "It pays to tell the truth." I found out later that Peggy's car had been reposed and she had to catch the bus to take her son to day care and take a bus from day care to work. The clincher was the day care didn't open until 7:00am. Peggy was due at work by 8:00; she was arriving at 8:45 on the dot. Once Peggy explained her situation, Mr. Pittman gave her a warning and called his wife and asked if it would be okay if Peggy used their extra car until she got everything squared away. Not only that, he encouraged Peggy to find out what she owed and let him know by the next morning and he would see what his church could do to help her out and she wouldn't have to pay it back. Who wouldn't want a boss like that?

The day is hectic, because everyone is having their new computer installed. I had to organize the project, so I've been running around like a mad woman. It's 11:45, they have two computers left to install and my phone rings. I think, what could possibly be wrong? "Good morning this is Passion." "Hey there beautiful, how are you today?" I sigh, but with relief that nothing was wrong with the computer project. "Oh, Terry, it's you." "You sound like you are disappointed," he said. "No, that's not it. I have just been swamped this morning. What's up?" He was answering someone that had come into his office, and then all I could hear was hurt in his voice as he expressed himself. "Passion, how are you going to make a brother feel? Did you forget about dinner tonight"? I placed my hand over my mouth and closed my eyes, because I had forgotten. "Oh my goodness Terry, I apologize I did forget. Not that I wouldn't have remembered later. I will still be there, 7:30 at the Lilac Café right?" "Yeah, that's right. Don't stand me up okay". "I won't, I'll be there."

I've been so busy today that I had forgotten about dinner. I will have to leave here and go straight to the Lilac, I'm sure I can find something to finish around here until then.

The last four hours of the day went by so quickly. I'm on my way to meet Terry and I can't even imagine what the night will be like. The last time I came to this café, was with Terry and that was the night we said our good-byes.

I arrived at the Lilac about fifteen minutes early, figuring I'd have some time to freshen up my make-up and my fragrance. As I lined my lips, there was a knock on my window. I was startled, but when I looked up there he was, in all of his splendor. Smooth dark chocolate skin; gorgeous smile; muscles bulging out everywhere; the whitest teeth known to man and the sexiest dimples on earth. I was smitten, lost for words completely zoned out. When I came to myself all I heard was, "Passion open the door." Terry was standing there laughing at me, but I couldn't say a word nor could I move. Listen, this man was more than fine; he was built like a Greek god. He was the total package. I managed to press the remote to unlock the car door. "Are you okay in there baby?" He asked, looking like a GQ model.

Finally, I was able to muster up a "yes". "Well, then why are you keeping me waiting? Come on and give me a hug." In my head I started screaming "Lord, please don't let this man touch me." It was too late, after putting my lip liner back into my purse I turned around and he was reaching for my hand. I placed my hand in his, stepped out of the car with my left foot adorned in a four inch bronze peep toe pump, and a fresh pedicure. My foot alone was bad. Meanwhile, Terry was reaching for my other hand. I slid my bronze colored Coach purse onto my shoulder and Terry stood me up like a prize trophy. I stepped to the side as he closed my car door. "My, my like fine wine girl you get better with time." "Yeah, whatever Terry, you still try to play the smooth role." I said. "Seriously Passion you look better than ever. You have always been a beautiful thick woman to me." "Thanks Terry, but can we go inside before lightening strikes?" "Oooh, I see how you're gonna play a brother. Come on our table is ready and waiting."

This place was as romantic as ever. Candles for lights on each table, a live jazz band playing and a young jazz vocalist, that sounded like velvet you had no choice but to relax. The atmosphere was perfect for the right soul mate. Terry and I walked over to our table; it was somewhat secluded yet in the heart of it all. He pulled the chair out for me; I sat down and quickly got comfortable. Terry removed his jacket and Lawd have mercy that clean white heavily starched button down shirt was well worn. His cuff links looked like five-karat diamonds. He was a well put together. He sat down and almost immediately our waiter came over to take our drink order. Terry said, "I'll have a rum and coke and the lady will have…. there was a pause, he looked at me and I nodded my head, he continued by saying "A Long Island Iced tea." The waiter left. Terry reached over and took both of my hands and looked me in my eyes and said, "I missed you so much girl. Why I suggested we take a break I'll never know." That brought back a painful moment. All I could say was "I don't know either." He kissed the back of my hand and I just knew I was going to pass out.

The band begins to play "Sweet Love", and it was so nice. The waiter brought us our drinks; Terry took a sip and began to talk. "Baby, I wanted to talk to you tonight because I would like to see you again exclusively. Just you and I like old times. I know this may seem like a lot all at once, so if you need time to think it over I'll understand."

This is exactly what I expected. Now, I have to figure out a way to let the brother down easy. Even though Terry was a good-looking man, settling down with him would never happen again. "Terry…."Wait, hold that thought" he says and he heads for the men's room. My phone rings at the same time. I didn't recognize the number but I answered anyway. "Hello, this is Passion." "Well, hello there lovely lady, how are you on this wonderful evening?" Oh my goodness it was Kris. In a shocked tone of voice I said, "I'm fine, thank you and yourself?" "I am doing well. Listen did I catch you at a bad time?" he asked. "Yes actually you did, I'm having dinner right now. Will it be too much trouble to ask you to give me a call at work tomorrow?" With complete understanding he said "Certainly, I'll be more than glad to call you tomorrow. Enjoy the remainder of your evening and I'll be praying for you." Wow, "praying for me", I thought to myself before responding. "Thanks, I really appreciate your understanding. I'll talk with you then, good-night." "Goodnight", he said and he hung up.

As soon as I put my phone back in my purse, Terry returns to the table. "Did you miss me?" I gave him a look that answered his question. "Terry, as I was saying before our brief interruption. I am really not ready to go back into a serious relationship. I am at a good place in my life and I want to maintain it. I really hope you understand and respect my decision." Of course, it was quiet for a minute, and then Terry said, "Yes, I respect your decision. Can we however, remain friends and maybe hang out every now and then?" "That's fine, I'd like to remain friends and I appreciate you not being upset about it."

The waiter came back, took our order and the band begin to play another song. Much to my surprise, Terry asked me to dance. We walked out onto the dance floor, he put his arms around me, held me close and it was over. He made me feel so safe. I couldn't help resting my head on his shoulder and getting a whiff of that awesome cologne he was wearing. I was like a baby in its mother's arms being rocked to sleep. I was very comfortable, and then all of a sudden he kissed me. This wasn't a peck either, it was a serious kiss. I pushed him away and walked off the dance floor. I was so confused. I enjoyed it, but at the same time I was angry. Terry ran after me. "Passion, what's the problem?" I turned around and looked at him with disgust and *lust* and said, "That's not what I want from you Terry. We just talked about that. I only want your friendship." The way he looked at me said he wasn't pleased with the way I reacted and he certainly verbalized it. "Girl, are you going to stand here and tell me you didn't enjoy that kiss at all or that you didn't even feel anything?" "Yes, I am," I quickly replied knowing full well that every bit of me was captured by that kiss. I had to maintain my stand on that though, because once again I'm not going to be consumed by lust for this man. "Passion, you were my lady for seven years and you expect me to believe what you're saying?" He was right, but of course I'll never tell. "Terry, you can believe what you want but I'm a changed woman now. I gave you up over a year ago and I'm not coming back." He looked at me with disgust and walked back to our table. The waiter had already bought our food to the table and he was waiting for us to come back. As soon as we walked up, he left. We ate our meal in silence. It appeared we were both ready to end the evening. Terry motioned for the waiter and when he got to the table Terry asked him for the check. When he bought it back, Terry gave him a credit card.

As we gathered our things, the waiter returned with Terry's receipt. He added the tip, signed it and we walked out. Once we reached the parking lot, Terry said, "I'll follow you home like I used to." He waited for me to get into my car, and then he got into his car. As we drove towards my house that was only ten minutes away, I begin to think about what Terry and I once had. He was always a gentleman and made sure I had whatever I needed. My parents didn't think so much of him, but I couldn't let go of him. My dad is and always has been a protector. He was going to ensure the safety of his family. When the relationship ended, it was hard for me. I think what hurt the most, was the fact that Terry had no real reason for ending everything. He said he just needed space. From the time we broke up until this very moment, I've never seen him with another woman nor have I even heard that he was with anyone else.

I pulled into the garage and Terry pulled into the driveway behind me. He walked with me into the house to make sure everything was okay. Before he left he said "Passion, I apologize if I offended you." I thought it sweet of him to apologize and I am a sucker for a polite man. Before I knew it, we were sharing a kiss. That old flame was instantly rekindled and I knew I was in trouble. "What have I done"?

CHAPTER THREE

The alarm went off. I turned over and there he was the thorn in my flesh. I kissed Terry on the forehead to wake him. He still had a few items boxed up at my place that he never picked up. He showered and changed in the guest bathroom, while I showered and dressed in my room. There was an awkward feeling in the air and neither one of us said much until we were about to leave. "Terry, about last night, I should never have done that. I don't know what came over me." He walked over to me and hugged me. "Don't worry baby, it will be alright. We only did what comes natural, when two people are in love." We left the house together and Terry said he would call me later.

The night danced through my head over and over again, not one thing that happened was supposed to happen. I am so upset with myself, because I know better. I let my guard down and now for the rest of the day, I'll be trapped in my imagination. I say I know better, because I have a relationship with God. I gave my life to Him when I was 10 years old and my parents always taught me the ways of God. Once I went off to college, I backslid. I guess that's why

Terry was and is such a big secret. No one knows that we have reconnected.

Finally, Friday is here. I am really ready for the weekend; there is so much going on in the city that no one has an excuse to be bored. There are no meetings scheduled for today, so I can do some filing and update Mr. Pittman's calendar. He has a rather large publishing conference next week and he likes everything to be in order. Our number one selling author will be there promoting, selling and signing her newest book. Maci Richards has churned out nothing but best sellers for the last three years, yet she is so humble and she never meets a stranger. She is a blessing.

It's already 11:00 am and just about time for lunch, I sure would like something good. I get up from my chair to go to my file cabinet and the receptionist buzzes me. "Yes, Cheryl". "Ms. Taylor, could you please come and sign for a package?" I'm a little puzzled because Cheryl can sign for any package that is delivered. "Can't you sign for it Cheryl?" "I would Ms. Taylor, but the sender said the package had to be signed for by you." I was really puzzled now. "By me," I said. "Yes, by you."

I put the files on top of the file cabinet and let Cheryl know I was on my way up to her desk. While I walked up to the front, I couldn't help noticing that Mr. Pittman's door was closed and it appeared he was meeting with someone. I had already checked his calendar and his next scheduled appointment wasn't until 1:00pm. Must be an employee I thought to myself. Oh, well. When I got to Cheryl's desk, I asked her, "What is so important?" She started smiling as a floral shop deliveryman came up behind me, with a dozen red and yellow roses. I was in shock. "Who would send me roses?" I thought to myself. I signed the pad, said "thank you" and he left me with the roses. Cheryl was so excited; you would've thought the roses were for her. She yells out, "Read the card!. I look at her and I calmly say, "Okay, give me a minute." I opened the card and it read: "To a very special lady, who holds a very special place in my heart". Love Ya, "T". Oh my goodness, they were from Terry. I have to nip this in the bud right now. All of a sudden I hear Cheryl as I walk off. "So, what does it say?" I just looked at her smiled and said, "Don't worry, it was nice". I turned away and walked as fast as I could down the hall back to my office, but not quite fast enough. As soon as I reached Mr. Pittman's office, his door opened and out walks Kris with Mr. Pittman following. "Ms. Taylor, good morning, you in a rush?" If I were fair skinned I would more than likely be as red as a beet right now. "No, sir just trying to put this vase down, it's a little heavy." I manage to muster up a smile. "Good morning Passion", Kris says. I reply softly, "Good morning". I felt so stupid. "Beautiful flowers, for a beautiful lady." "Thanks". Mr. Pittman looks on in bewilderment. "Ms. Taylor", he says. "Do you know my nephew Kris?" Inside, I begin to scream so loud, that I started to shake. "Your nephew? I had no idea". We literally bumped into one another in the hallway after the last monthly meeting we had. So, I guess you can say we know one another." Talk about being in a bad position. "Let me take those for you", Kris offered as he reached to take the flowers from me. I managed to pull the note card out before he could see it and without him noticing. "Thanks", I said. He responded with, "Not a problem, you're welcome. Have you made any plans for lunch already?" Internally I grabbed my head, and thought what is going on. I can't go out again with my bosses' nephew, that won't work. I quickly responded, "Yes, I'm sorry I do. I have to run an errand, before I grab a bite." The expression on Kris' face was one of disbelief, but he simply said, "That's fine, I understand. If it's okay with you, can I give you a call later on this evening?" "Sure Kris", I said. "That will be fine." Kris walked out of the office and out into the parking lot. I went into my office and stood in the window and watched him as he walked to his car. He got into his car, but never drove off he just sat there. I began to wonder if he was waiting to see if I was really going to lunch alone. "What is he doing?"

Kris sits in his car and begins to pray: *"Dear Lord I come to you today, thanking you for the relationship I have with you. I understand your word says, if I delight myself in you, you would give me the desires of my heart. I come to pour my heart out to you today. I've come to thank you for Passion Taylor. Thank you for allowing me to bump into her in the hallway. I pray that you would cover and protect her, cause her to recognize the devil when he is at work and run from him. Preserve her oh, God. There are so many awesome qualities I see in her, that would make her an incredible wife. Touch her Lord and turn her heart towards me. Cause her to prosper in every area of her life as her relationship with you grows. Father, you have kept me since Melanie's death, now I'm growing fond of Passion and my heart has now found a new love. Mold her and make her and when the time is right Lord, present her to me for a lifetime. I thank you for hearing and answering my prayer, in Jesus' name I pray, Amen."*

Finally, Kris pulls off. I felt really bad for lying to him. I just needed some time to myself to think some things over. I turned away from my window and headed towards my desk and immediately I am faced with the reality of Terry. I am thinking of what I should say to him when I call. The flowers he sent me are beautiful and he is a wonderful man, but I can't allow myself to be distracted. I just rededicated my life to Christ and I want to maintain my relationship with Him. I am going to need the strength of God, to overcome this thorn in my flesh.

I left for lunch and since I told Kris I had to run an errand, I did. I went to a Christian bookstore that I had heard so much about and browsed around. I saw several things that I wanted to buy, but I realized I could only read one book at a time. So, I decided on a new bible, a CD and one other book. I made my purchase and went into the café attached to the bookstore. I sat down and ordered a sandwich, chips and a drink. I took out my new bible and begin to thumb through it. There were a ton of study helps and notes. I could have sat there all day, but I couldn't I had to get back to the office. I finished my lunch and left.

Once I got back to my office, I started filing again and getting things back in order. It is my heart's desire to become much closer to God. I have a cousin that lives in Phoenix, her name is Samaria and she has such an awesome relationship with God. I would love to walk with God like she does. We use to tease her a lot about how much she loved God, when we were teenagers, because she was so different. She wasn't into the same things we were into. Can you imagine being sixteen and loving God? God was Samaria's best friend. She was a strong girl; I watched her deal with a father that was an alcoholic. When she'd had enough, she prayed and God delivered him. I've also seen her rise above a broken marriage. You would think God would have given her a break, since she dealt with her father in such a Godly manor. Her husband Mitchell was saved to, so he said. Samaria found out other wise when she learned that Mitchell had been cheating. Yup, he cheated and more than once. They went to counseling and he still cheated. I couldn't have done it. Samaria remained faithful to that clown though.

She prayed, fasted and didn't talk about it. Her not talking, meant that if anyone ministered to her about her marriage she would know for sure it was God. She stood on the scripture Exodus 14:14 and yes, God did fight for her. I have to say I was blown away, as we all watched as God changed Mitchell from head to toe. It was no one but God that could have made such changes in Mitchell's life. The thing that was so interesting about Samaria was, when she was praying she was praying for God to change her into a "Proverbs 31" woman. Her prayers weren't about Mitchell cheating it was about their souls. She told me if her husband ended up lost it was like her being lost to. Well, it paid off God has blessed their marriage tremendously. Mitchell has rededicated his life to Christ and his wife. He publicly made it known that he only had eyes and love for his wife and God. He asked Samaria to please forgive him for all he had done and said to her. Samaria being who she is, forgave him and they moved forward. Today I can say they are truly happy and in love. God turned their relationship around for real.

I've heard Samaria speak about being accountable and I would like for her to tell me more about it. I really admire her and she has no idea about the effect she has had on my life. I thank God for her.

"Buzz, buzz", the sound of my intercom and me being paged by Cheryl. "Yes, Cheryl". "Excuse me Ms. Taylor, but there's a gentleman here to see you". Someone to see me? I'm not expecting anyone I thought to myself. "Did he give you a name Cheryl?" Whispering, she says "Yes, Terry St. James". I pause for a moment, "I'll be right out Cheryl". I hang up and question myself about what Terry could want. I didn't want to jump to conclusions, so I collected my thoughts and went out front with a smile.

Trying to keep this on a professional level, I don't greet Terry like a friend I greet him like a client. "Good afternoon Mr. St. James, I'm sorry I wasn't expecting you." Terry looks at me like I have totally lost my mind, but responds. "Thank you Ms. Taylor, I am glad you could see me", as he reaches to shake my hand. "Follow me please", I said. We turn and walk down the hall, with me leading the way. Terry follows closely behind enjoying the view. Awful isn't it?

When we reach my office, I stand to the side as Terry walks in. I take a quick look down the hall towards Mr. Pittman's office, to make sure he was occupied. When I closed the door and turned around, Terry is right in my face. I'm speechless and he kisses me. The sad thing is I don't stop him. Terry holds me so tight; I could feel the blood flowing quickly through his veins. We stop, look at one another and realize we have to pull it together. Terry speaks first, "Girl, I've been missing you and wanting to see you. The thought of you makes me smile and if I have to wait to long to see you, I get a serious attitude. What I had for you Passion never died. You're the ray to my sunshine; the lyrics to my song; the beat to my heart and the connection to my soul. You are what I want and you're more than what I need. You're my refreshing breeze on a nice hot summer day. I love you girl." I was speechless. I know I should wait and pray before getting back into this relationship, but it just feels so good. I think I'm in too deep now, but I'm sure I can control how things go this time.

"Listen, Terry I think we need to slow down, we are moving way to fast. We really need to think about what we are doing". Terry took his hand and rubbed it across his mouth before he said, "Look Passion, I'm in this all the way and I don't want to wait, I want you. Do you want me or not?"

I couldn't say anything. This was going too fast for me. I wanted it, but at the same time I didn't want it. I looked at him and slightly nodded my head "yes".

CHAPTER FOUR

I thought the weekend would never get here but I am so glad it is. As I lay here looking at my ceiling, I started thinking about my best friend Samantha. She passed away about six months ago. We had known one another since kindergarten. She was only thirty-four years old and she died in her sleep. She wasn't sick or anything. It has been said that she died from a broken heart. I know that she was sad, but not sad enough to die. Samantha's father did some not so nice things to her for many years. He was a very popular preacher and her mother never did anything about what happened. All of the members that left the church said the First Lady was only concerned about having a nice wardrobe, car, house and money in her designer bags. Not about her daughter's well being. Samantha left the church when she went off to college and never went back; at least not there. She joined our church, received her healing and actually went to see her father and told him she forgave him. She knew that God would take care of him for what he had done.

If Samantha were alive, she would be truthful with me about Terry. She'd say, "Girl, go for it", or "Passion, let that him go he's not good for you." I really miss her.

Tears begin to roll down my face. Terry comes into the bedroom, he asks, "Honey, what's wrong?" I paused for a moment, "I was just thinking about Samantha." Terry knew Samantha, because we all went to Mathis University together. "I know you miss her baby, but hang in there you will get better with time". He always said the right thing at the right time.

Terry had gotten dressed and was about to head out and play golf with some of his buddies. Being the Vice President of a bank, you can do that. We planned to take in a movie later this evening. With Terry gone I was able to tidy up the house. I really didn't have any plans for today, so I was excited about having time alone.

I was heading down the hall to the laundry room, when my phone rang. I picked up and said, "Good morning". The party on the other end hung up. I guess they had the wrong number or didn't want to talk. I went into the laundry room took the load out of the washing machine, put it in the dryer and put the last load in the washing machine.

I have finally trained myself to stay on task. That was a challenge for me. If I was cleaning the kitchen, went into the den to see if there were any glasses in there and saw anything out of place I'd start cleaning the den. That went on for a while until I pulled it together.

I went to the guest bathroom, to hang up new hand towels. As I walked down the hall, the phone rang again. This time they just got an aggravated "Hello".

"Good morning Passion, this is Kris. How are you on this fine Saturday?" I was certainly not expecting this phone call, but I sure was happy to get it. "I'm fine Kris, how about you?" I sat down on the sofa in the den and chatted for a while. Conversing with Kris was always refreshing. "I am blessed. Glad to have a weekend free. I travel a lot and whenever I am at home it's a joy. What's going on with you today?" That wasn't a hard question. "Nothing until a little later this evening" I said. Apparently shocked at my answer Kris said, "Wow, you're available today? Would you like to catch a movie around 2:30 this afternoon?" I thought about the fact that Terry and I were going to the movies later, but there was a slim chance he'd pick the same movie. "Okay, that's fine. What theatre?" I heard Kris typing on his computer before he answered, "Blair Towers". That theatre was in an affluent area of the city. I was quite impressed. We decided to meet at the church, park my car and ride in his car to the theatre. The women's ministry would be there in all night prayer, so the cars would be safe. We ended our call because I had to complete the task at hand.

It was about 11:45am and we were meeting at 1:15pm at the church. I finished up in the bathroom took a shower and got dressed. My clothes were already out for tonight, so that was half the battle.

The drive to the church from my house was thirty minutes, so I left at 12:15. It was a beautiful day and I was enjoying the drive, listening to a CD. I was also thinking about what this day with Kris was going to be like. He was quite different from Terry. They are both very nice men and very handsome I might add, but Terry really doesn't respect my wishes. "Why am I seeing him?" I often ask myself. If he really cared for me he'd help me by not being so seductive. That also means following me home but not coming in. "Who am I kidding?" I am just as much at fault as Terry is and the devil doesn't make me do it. I have to maintain control and just walk away. "What is wrong with me?" Am I really saved or am I deceiving myself?

My drive seemed shorter than usual; before I knew it I was there. Just as I suspected, Kris was there waiting. He didn't notice that I had pulled into the parking lot; it looked like he was preoccupied. I found a parking space, took a quick look in my rearview mirror to make sure everything was in place before I got out of the car. I walked up to the window of Kris' car, a black 700 series BMW and saw that he was reading. He had not noticed that I was standing there. I leaned in a little closer and noticed that he was reading the word. I couldn't make out what he was reading though. I went ahead and knocked on the window it startled him a little but he managed to muster up that gorgeous smile of his.

"Hi there", he said. "I'm sorry I didn't realize you were here, I was catching up on some reading. I have been studying Proverbs and I have to say it has been a blessing. I hope you haven't been here long." I thought I'd toy with him, "Well, I've been waiting for about 30 minutes". Kris began to apologize and I begin to laugh. I had to stop him. "I'm just kidding Kris, I just got here". "What did he do?" He smiled and said, "You got jokes?" We laughed. He got out of the car, walked around and opened the door for me to get in. I got in, buckled up and was ready for the ride. The seats in that car were amazing, the way they hugged me made me feel like I was in a spa. Kris got in and turned on some wonderful worship music. It was so peaceful in his car, not to mention I didn't have to deal with fighting my flesh or fighting him off. It was wonderful! I'm glad Kris called and invited me to the movies. This is going to be great!

While driving Kris looked over at me and said, "Passion, I'm so glad we're going to spend this afternoon together. I hope what I'm about to say won't come off as offensive, but I find myself thinking about you more and more lately". I'm thinking to myself does that bother me, are you kidding? The words finally vocalized, "No, that doesn't bother me at all. I find it sweet and surprising at the same time". Kris looked relieved, like he wanted to tell me that for a long time. He continued, "I enjoy the time I spend with you and I can't imagine why you would be surprised. You have never given me a reason not to want to share time with you. You've always presented yourself in a ladylike manor." In the back of my mind, I thought if he only knew. I am not that ladylike woman he thinks I am. "Kris, you have to know I'm human and I do have issues or should I say some "skeletons"? Everyone does and sometimes it's best that we don't open the closet door." He thought for a moment and followed with an "Amen".

We arrived at the movie theatre, went in purchased our tickets, ordered our popcorn, drinks and twizzlers. The crowd wasn't very large at all so that made it easy to pick a good seat. We had about five minutes before the movie started so we made sure we had everything we needed sat down and got comfortable. We chatted a little more while eating some popcorn, then all of a sudden out of nowhere in walked a mob of people. I am so glad we arrived when we did. We looked at one another and burst out laughing. At least the seats on both sides of us remained empty.

The movie had been on for about forty-five minutes and it was getting good when my phone vibrated. It was a text message from Terry. It read, "Sorry, something came up and we will have to reschedule. Love ya." I probably should have felt bad but I didn't. There will be a next time with Terry, but right now I want to enjoy the movie and my time with Kris.

The movie was great! Before it ended, you could hear sniffles throughout the entire theatre. Yes, it was a tearjerker. When Kris and I walked out to the car, he slipped me a tissue to wipe my tears away. He also started laughing because he thought it was cute. I was thinking, what's wrong with showing a little emotion?

Once Kris started driving, he said "Where to next?" I figured I'd try my hand at a little humor with him, "What do you mean next?" I said. "We were only supposed to be going to the movies and that's it." The look on Kris' face was one of total shock. I could tell he was searching for the right words to reply, but I just couldn't let him suffer any longer. "Got cha", I blurted out. Kris looked at me as he began to slow down and pull over; he unlocked the doors and said, "Get out!" The tone he said it in was so brash. I couldn't believe he was angry. "Kris I...." he cut me off, "You what Passion? You must have been about to say you're rude, because that's what you are. Now please get out." It was totally silent as he tapped on his steering wheel. With tears in my eyes I meekly said, "I apologize" and put my hand on the door handle, when Kris started laughing hysterically. I looked at him and he said, "Now, who got who?" and continued to laugh. I couldn't even get upset, because I started it. I just picked my face up off the floor and joined in on the laughter.

CHAPTER FIVE

After we finally calmed down, we decided to go to the local museum and check out the featured exhibit. The exhibit was called, *"The Expressions of the Young"* and it was so touching. There were photographs of small children, all sizes, shapes and colors. They were absolutely adorable. Each one of them wore a different but yet unique expression on their face. One was crying, one was laughing hysterically, one was smiling, one was angry, one was sad and one was confused. Nonetheless, they were all cute.

The photographer, Lindley Habersham was at the exhibit walking amongst the guest introducing herself. She was very cordial and passionate about her work; she gave Kris and I a business card and thanked us for coming. We walked around for a few more minutes and then headed across the street to the park.

It was such a beautiful day and I was enjoying myself so much. I could actually say something about God's handy work right here, but it wouldn't involve the trees, birds or flowers it would only involve the handsome young man I was walking next to in the park, Kris. I know I have only been out with Kris a few times, but he is an amazing man and I don't want to mess things up.

Kris and I sat on the park bench talking, as we watched people walk by; ride their bikes; roller-skate and push their kids in a stroller, while jogging. Every now and again a couple would walk by holding holds, smiling and talking. I could picture Kris and I doing that very same thing, but I have to put the brakes on it and slow down a bit. I have to control my thoughts about him, we are just friends and moving beyond that isn't in the picture.

Kris and I talked a lot about what we wanted in our natural life as well as what we wanted spiritually. I could be real about my spiritual desires with Kris, because he seems to understand the love I have for God. Terry on the other hand, was all about the flesh. I can't say he was in it alone, because I did enjoy every single moment I was with him. Even though I knew it was wrong. I just had to be with him. I always hear people in church talk about their horrible life of sin. "What took them so long to be delivered if it was so bad?" They know they loved every minute of it. I don't know about anyone else, but I like George Washington, "cannot tell a lie".

I was so enjoying the time I was spending with Kris, but I was not willing to allow my flesh to take over.

There were several times I would look at him and it wasn't in a prayerful way. I had to take control.

Kris saw an ice cream stand and we walked over and got a couple of cones. He had vanilla and I had pralines and cream. Talk about delicious. As Kris was enjoying his cone, he stopped and said, "Today has turned out to be really nice. It would be great if it didn't have to end." I smiled slightly and said, "It doesn't; besides my other plans were cancelled." His face lit up. "Great, would you like to go to dinner?" "Sure, that sounds fine", I said. He suggested we go to the church and pick up my car. We would choose a restaurant and we would we meet there later. That way we could both leave after dinner and go straight home.

It was about 5:40pm when Kris dropped me off at the church. I had a plan mapped out. I would go choose something to wear, shower, relax for a few minutes, get dressed and leave. I had just finished ironing when my doorbell rang. I was not expecting anyone, so I couldn't imagine who it might be. I looked through the peephole and there stood my sister Precious. I opened the door and she was standing there crying her eyes out.

Immediately I thought something was wrong with our parents. "Precious, come on in. What's going on? Is something wrong with Mom and Dad?" She didn't answer, she just cried. I asked her again and she still didn't say anything. Finally, I went into the den and got the cordless phone and started dialing my parents' phone number. "Who are you calling?" Precious asked through her tears. "Mom and Dad", I said. She motioned for me to hang up and I did. Now maybe we could get to the bottom of this.

"Precious, what is going on?" She looked at me, dropped her head and sadly said, "Brad broke up with me, what am I going to do?" I stood there looking back at her remembering Mom, Dad and I telling Precious that Brad was up to no good. I would not dare say, "I told you so", instead I said, "What do you mean, what are you going to do?" I continued. "What you're going to do is, get your things and move in here. You can stay here for as long as you need to. You have family so we are going to help you pick up the pieces and move on past Brad". She seemed puzzled. It was like she was expecting me to say more than that. I didn't have to because she already knew the deal, besides it wouldn't be a good thing to kick her while she was already down.

She was much calmer now than she was when she first came over. Softly, she said, "Passion, the only reason I asked what am I going to do, is because I'm pregnant. That's why Brad broke up with me. Now all of a sudden, I've been cheating on him. I can't believe, some of the things that came out of his mouth towards me". Okay, so now I am completely speechless. "Pregnant"! I yelled.   Quickly, I pulled myself together and thought about what I was going to say next.   I spoke, "Precious, listen I'm getting ready to go out for a while.   You are more than welcome to stay here, grab a bite to eat and take a nap.   We'll talk more tomorrow.   I love you girl and I'll help you work through this.   We will come up with a plan and go from there.   I gave her a hug, finished getting dressed and left.

Once I got on the highway, I started thinking about Precious, my baby sister a mother.   I know this will shock my parents so I may as well plan to go with Precious to tell them.   She's a bright young lady who got caught up in the thought of loving a guy who wasn't ready to settle down.   I know Precious, at the on set of a crisis she panics but she can take a bad situation and turn it into success.   She'll be just fine.   I smile and think to myself, I'm going to be an Aunt.   I certainly am not justifying Precious being pregnant out of wedlock, but I can't just throw her away either.   As family and a Christian, I will have to love Precious and ensure she has a relationship with Christ.   Besides, her baby should grow up in a Christian environment.

Before I knew it, I was there.   It was Saturday night and we decided to go to a sports café called "First Down".   It was down town and was always crowded will all sorts of sports fans.   A good basketball game was coming on, the Los Angeles Lakers –vs.- the

Boston Celtics. I most certainly am not a Lakers fan, I love myself some Boston Celtics and "Rajon Rondo". Good thing for Kris that he does to. I got out of my car and walked to the entrance, Kris was standing there waiting for me. "Wow", he said. "You look wonderful." I had to play the modest role. "Thanks, but this outfit is really old." I had on a pair of straight leg boot cut jeans, dark blue. Black ankle boots with a two inch heel, a black lace front camisole and a black blazer. Kris started laughing at me, just like he did this afternoon then he said, "You know you look good girl, that's why you picked that outfit. Your modesty is nice though." I couldn't say a word. We went to our table and ordered some chicken wings, onion rings and sweet tea. All of the big screen TV's were on and the café began to get crowded. Fans came in with their team attire on and the crowd was pumped up and ready to go.

As the night progressed, Kris and I laughed, gave one another high fives, ate and simply enjoyed ourselves. This kind of fun was good and I knew the night would not end with regrets.

The game was over and the Celtics won. The atmosphere was still charged. Kris and I sat and talked for a little while longer. We were more relaxed with one another and not so much trying to impress. I think I could be more than friends with him. Just as my thought concluded Kris turns to me and says, "I

44

am really enjoying being out with you tonight." I smiled and said, "Same here." He reached over and took my hand. My heart started racing, Kris had warm, soft yet firm hands. When he touched me, it was so different. I felt an unusual peace and so very safe. It was quite nice.

Kris walked me to my car, gave me a nice long hug and made sure I was in the car safely. I waited while he got into his car, before I drove off. Once he was in his car he flashed his headlights and we drove off together.

As I drove home, the fact that Kris was becoming special to me crossed my mind. I wondered more, of what he thought of me. Should I pray and ask God for more? Is that the right thing for a lady to do? My pleasant thoughts were interrupted by a text message. "What could Princess want?" I said out loud to myself. I hope she doesn't think I am going to run around for anything she is craving. The text read: "Hey where are you coming from so late?" It was Terry, I had not heard from him in a minute and all of a sudden he texts me. "Who's asking?" I texted back. He replied with, "You know who this is, your number one man – Terry". I texted him back and asked him to call me. A few seconds later, my phone rang. "Hello". After my greeting Terry begins to speak. "Where are you?" He demanded. I was a tad bit irritated because I felt he was wrong and had no right to question me.

"I am on my way home", I replied with a little attitude. "Home", he snapped. "At this late hour?" "Excuse me", I said. "What gives you the right, to question my where abouts?" I waited for an answer and I'm not sure I should have. "Just being Terry gives me that right. I mean we are an item and I can ask my woman where she is any time I want." I paused for a moment and then I let him have it. "What do you mean, we are an item? I figure if we are an item then I would see more of you and certainly hear from you more often than when it fits into your schedule." I didn't stop there, I kept on going. "Terry days or weeks go by and I don't hear from you. How can we be an item when we aren't even in love and don't communicate?" I am tired of this counterfeit relationship and I need to move on." Instead of waiting for a response I hung up the phone. By that time I was pulling into my driveway and singing a new song in my head. It went a little something like this, wanna hear it? Here it go. "I finally let him go and now I feel brand new." It doesn't have a lot of words and it doesn't need to. I am free from the bondage of my past and I only want God's best for me. The devil has a way to try and keep God's people trapped, but I refuse to let him make a fool out of me.

I went into the house, peeped in on Precious only to find her knocked out. I took my shower singing my song, got dressed, prayed read the word and asked God to please order my steps. As I lay down in the bed, I realized I needed some answers and I needed them fast.

CHAPTER SIX

This will be a busy week, we have two training sessions at work and I have to help put the manuals together and schedule the caterers for lunch. Mr. Pittman is a great boss and he wants everything done in the spirit of excellence. I have a few more calls to make before we set up the training room. "Good morning Passion." I was in the break room getting coffee cups and hot chocolate, when I heard someone speak. I turned around and Peggy was standing there with a large smile on her face. I said, "Good morning Peggy, how are you today?" She responded with "I'm doing great, thanks for asking." Peggy was always cheerful, no matter what was going on in her life. She was a great person to work with. "Passion, could you use some extra help?" She asked. I was not turning down any help so I of course said, "Yes" so quick it would make someone's head swim. Peggy and I set up the coffee maker, cups, napkins, doughnuts and danishes. When the meeting started and everyone came in they could just help themselves. I thanked Peggy for all of her help and went back to my office to order the lunches.

Before I knew it, it was 9:00am. Employees were going to the training room taking their seats and our facilitators were checking in at the front desk with

Cheryl. She buzzed me when they were all here. I went up greeted them, made sure they all had their visitors badges and walked them back to Mr. Pittman's conference room.

Now that the training session has started, I have a couple of hours to myself. I can catch up on some things that I need to have done for next week. I'll do as much as I can until they break for lunch at noon. All of a sudden there was a knock on my office door. "Come in." It was Cheryl; she stuck her head in and said, "You have a package. I already signed for it, just dropping it off." She brings in a beautiful bouquet of flowers and a box of chocolates. I think to myself, "Terry". "Thanks Cheryl", I said. I hurry and tear open the card and it reads; "I thank God daily for bringing you into my life. I pray you have a wonderful day. Love ya, Kris." Wow, my heart is beating so fast and I am left breathless. We did have a great time over the weekend, but these flowers and chocolates are such a surprise. Another knock at my office door, I answer with some frustration in my voice. "Yes". Cheryl opens the door and says "So". I replied, "So what?" She says, "Who is being so sweet to you?" I hesitated before speaking and said, "A very dear friend." Cheryl read between the lines and said, "I guess that's your way of being polite and saying none of my business." I laughed and at the same time, I was thinking "Yup, you're right."

After Cheryl left, I sat back in my seat and thought about those flowers from Kris and if I should call him.

I know I should thank him, but I don't want to seem too excited. Right then my phone rang. "Hello", I said. "Good morning Sunshine, how are you?" My heart begin to flutter, it was Kris. "Hi there Kris, I was just about to call and say thank you for the candy and the lovely flowers." "You are quite welcome. I hope it wasn't too much. I really had a great time over the weekend and I wanted you to know that." In my mind I was thinking, where have you been all my life. "That was so sweet of you; maybe we can do it again sometime." "I would love to do it again this weekend, but I will be out of town." All of a sudden I was a little down. I couldn't believe it, I was feeling stronger for Kris and I didn't want him to go away. "Well", I said, "Maybe we can go out when you come back." Kris laughed a little and said, "That will be something to look forward to." I followed by saying, "It will be."

Monday nights are usually quiet for me. I go home, cook something simple, take a long bath or shower, put on my old college tee shirt and shorts, eat and then curl up with a good book or watch a good movie. Tonight I think I'll watch a movie. I forgot one important thing; Precious is staying with me now. It has been fine so far and she has pretty much kept to herself or been asleep. Maybe we can spend some sister time together.

I was finally home and I was glad about it. Precious was there and I was excited about spending some time with her. I went into the house and decided to cook shrimp, steak, salad and baked potatoes for dinner. I seasoned the steaks and put them in the oven, seasoned the shrimp in a bowl, covered them with plastic wrap and put them in the refrigerator. I was thinking I would sauté them to eat as appetizers. I washed the potatoes, rubbed them with some oil, sprinkled salt on them and put them in the oven. I put the salad mix in a bowl and in the fridge.

I went into my room, undressed put on my bathrobe, started my bath water and went to knock on my sister's room door. After I knocked, I heard a faint "Come in". I opened the door slowly and went in. Precious was buried beneath the covers. "Are you okay?" I asked. She answered again faintly, "Headache". I paused for a moment and I asked, "You feel like having dinner with me?" She mustered up enough energy to hold up her head and say, "You bet I do". I told her to get up and put on something and once I got out of the tub, I'd finish dinner and we could eat. She agreed.

Everything looked delicious and we were about to dig in when the doorbell rang. I looked at Precious and she said "Don't look at me; I'm not expecting anyone right now." Looking down, at her stomach. I laughed, went and looked through the peephole; much to my surprise, someone I absolutely was not expecting was standing there. In the background I could hear Precious saying, "Well, who is it?" I opened the door and there she stood. It was my cousin, Samaria.

"Hey there cuz," she said in the loud energetic way only she could do. She continued. "Stop looking all shocked and let's get this bag in the house." She walked in and I took her bag. Yes, I was shocked. I was in no way upset though, because I had been thinking of calling and talking to her about Kris and Terry. She went over hugged Precious rubbed her belly and said, "We'll talk later." Precious gave her an "Oh, no" look. I was looking in amazement that she just showed up.

"What's up family?" She says. All I can do is just laugh. She is the only family member I know that loves God and can come at you, with a "Praise the Lord Saints" or a "What up yo?" Samaria always makes me laugh and she doesn't understand why. She doesn't think she is funny at all, but I tell her that she is an undercover comedian. I'll have to video tape her and let her see herself in action.

In response to her question "What up family?" I said, "Not much" and she came back with a common Samaria remark, "Not praying, uh?" I knew not to laugh at that, because she was serious. Precious on the other hand had to say something. "Why we always have to not be doing something?" "You seem to be keeping pretty busy cuz", Samaria replied, while looking over her glasses at Precious' belly. "Very funny", Precious grunted.

I helped Samaria put her things in the guest room. She took the time to change into something a little more comfortable and joined us for dinner. I am so glad that I cooked all three steaks and baked two extra potatoes. I wasn't sure if Precious would want more. We had plenty of shrimp and salad so that wasn't a worry.

It was great seeing my cousin, I was glad she surprised me and came to visit. We finished dinner, cleaned up the kitchen and went in the den to sit down and talk. Precious said "good night", gave each of us a hug and headed off to bed.

I couldn't bring myself to talk to Samaria about Terry and Kris, because I knew she would have something deep to say. Then all of a sudden out of the blue it happened, she asked, "So, what's up with the two guys in your life? You know the ones you are wrestling with in your spirit?" She absolutely freaks me out when she does that. I know she prays for me; I know God speaks to her; I believe she loves me and obeys God by helping me settle my issues. It still doesn't change the fact that I feel like she's reading my mind. I guess this is as a good a time as any to go on and discuss it and get her take on it. I began…."Remember Terry?" Samaria looked at me and said "You mean that want to be playboy?" I laughed, but I knew it was the truth and my response couldn't be anything but "Yes". I continued filling her in. "Terry and I had a good relationship and for reasons of his, we broke up. It wasn't a bitter break up but it did hurt. Well, after a long time, and I do mean a long time he pops back up and so do my feelings. However, I've met a new guy. His name is Kris, he is so sweet and he loves God with all of his heart. I can't for the life of me, seem to get over Terry though. There was a nice long pause. "Well, Passion you know where I am going to go with this. First of all, you should wait on God. No relationship will work, if you move off of your feelings. You have to know beyond the shadow of a doubt that God has ordained your relationship. You have some decisions to make and only you can make them. They can't be based on the opinions of others you know. It will take you fasting and seeking the face of God to get a sure answer." I sat in silence for a minute to gather my words carefully, and then I spoke. "You make it sound so easy Samaria. You've been saved for quite some time, so it's easy for you to reach out to God and get answers. I am still in the beginning stages, not to mention that I don't pray as often as you do. I have a long way to go." Samaria looked at me smiled and said, "You can do this Passion, you have to. No one can give the answers but God. He can use me or anyone else; you however, have to seek Him for yourself. Praying isn't a hard thing to do; you just have to do it. When you have a bill that you know you're going to pay late, you call the company to let them know, right?" I answered, "Yes". "Okay, then you can use that same faith to call on God for your everyday situations knowing He loves you and He will take care of you. The company you owe money to doesn't and won't."

Talks like these, are one of the reasons why I love her so much.

We sat and talked for a few more minutes, before Samaria prayed. Once she was done, we sat in the presence of God and couldn't do anything else after that but weep and go to sleep. I have to say, I slept well.

As I drove into work, I begin to think about what Samaria said and about my life as a Christian. I know my relationship with Jesus Christ needed to be stronger and more personal. I wasn't reading the bible like I should and I definitely wasn't praying like I should. I want more.

I have a beautiful home, a great job, a wonderful wardrobe and being a plus sized woman, I don't have a problem with getting a date. I just don't have a close relationship with God. I want what Samaria has. I know she has told me not to want what others have, because you never know what they went through to get it. She's right, but I want the devil himself to hate to see me wake up in the morning, because of the anointing on my life. I know that's how he feels when Samaria gets up. That's power and you only get that when you have a personal relationship with God.

When I reached the office I was off and running. The phone started ringing, requests were pouring in and all I could do was think about bible study tonight.

Was I becoming a "church girl" or what? Up until recently I used to think about going out on a date, going home or anything else but going to church. Something was happening; I could feel myself wanting to be closer to God. There was a change taking place; it must be the prayers of Samaria at work. When she has a prayer assignment, there will be results. I still wanted to be with Terry and he was not good for me. What am I going to do?

The day was actually going by pretty fast and I was glad about that. I walked out of my office into the hallway, headed to Mr. Pittman's office, to see if he needed anything. As I got close to his office, I noticed his door was ajar and he was talking to someone. I didn't want to appear to be eavesdropping, so I turned around to go back to my office and Peggy was coming in my direction. She looked to be in a bit of a hurry and going to Mr. Pittman's office. She passed by and smiled. I was a bit confused; I thought I was Mr. Pittman's assistant. Since when did he call Peggy in to do anything for him? When I went into my office, I turned and looked back and Peggy closed the door. I was thinking what was going on? Did I do something wrong? I sat down in my chair and begin to trace my steps from the start of the day; making sure I did all I was suppose to do. Then I thought it's probably nothing, I'm over reacting. Mr. Pittman is more than likely just discussing some front office business with her.

CHAPTER SEVEN

I was startled out of my thinking by a knock at my office door. I took a moment to get myself together before answering. I finally did answer, by saying, "Come in". I was so shocked to see Kris walk through the door.

When he came in the office he appeared to have something on his mind. "Good morning beautiful", he said. "How is your day going so far?" I immediately begin to think about Peggy in Mr. Pittman's office, but quickly pulled it together and said, "All is well, busy as usual. What brings you by the office today?" "I had to speak to my Uncle and see you as well." See me, what could he have to speak to me about, that would cause him to drive almost an hour to this office. "What's up?" I said. He began, "Well, Passion I wanted to invite you to a function at my parent's house next weekend. They are celebrating 40 years of marriage and I would love for you to be a part by accompanying me." I stood there in awe, just shocked. "Wow", is the first thing that came out of my mouth. Then I finished. "I find this invitation to truly be an honor and I would love to accompany you. I'm sure there are other women you could have asked, but thank you for choosing me." He had the largest smile I'd ever seen on his face. He looked at me and said, "Thank you Passion for accepting my invitation, I really appreciate it." Of course I was smiling as well from ear to ear. Okay, straight cheesing. I stopped long enough to ask Kris if he was going to bible study, and he was. We decided we'd meet one another there and possibly go out for coffee after.

By now I'm on cloud nine and so ready for the day to come to an end. I don't have long and I will surely make a mad dash for the door, when that clock strikes 5:00pm. Don't get me wrong, I love my job but when it's time to go, it's time to go. Back to life, phones are still ringing and business must go on as usual.

I had a training conference to plan, so I was clicking away on the Internet doing some research and putting my power point presentation together, when I realized it was 4:50pm. I started saving documents and putting files away so I could make my way to the church. I had such a strong feeling about the service tonight.

Kris and I met at the church at 6:45pm. Prayer starts at 7:00pm and we went straight in because we wanted to be on time. We made small talk as we walked in.

Once inside, I put my things on the seat next to Chris and went and knelt down at the altar. I began to tell God "Thank You", for everything; my job, my home, my family, my health and my strength. The saints were worshipping all around me and I felt so safe. There was a tugging in my spirit and I just started to cry. I wasn't sure what was going on, but I was willing to let it happen. It was as if

someone had turned on a water faucet. I just could not stop crying. The tears were coming and all I could do was moan. Then all of a sudden it happened, I began to speak in tongues. I know, I was up in age and had never spoken, but I was excited about it finally happening. My stomach muscles tightened up and I bent over and wrapped my arms around myself. Someone came and knelt down beside me, they didn't say a word they just put their arm around me. I felt so free; it was like everything I was carrying was being released. I was refreshed, renewed and revived. I could hear the saints around me saying "Breakthrough Lord", that was so what I wanted. Then I heard Pastor in the mic. He began to pray and just when I thought I was done crying, I started all over again. I lie down on the floor and let go even more. God was doing a new thing in me and I welcomed it. More than anything, I wanted a stronger relationship with Him. Maybe now I would have it.

When I finally got up, I saw that it was Samaria kneeling down beside me. Pastor ended up not teaching, but carrying the service out with prayer.

Samaria helped me to a pew and as I wiped my eyes, I looked around and saw Kris lying out on the floor weeping before God. All of a sudden I started crying again. I over heard Samaria tell Precious, she would drive me home in my car and she gave Precious the keys to drive her car. I don't really remember anything after that.

When my alarm went off for work, I got up to take my shower. When I looked in the mirror my eyes were so swollen, I looked like I had been in a fight. I got in the shower and still felt the power of God all over me. The move of God was so awesome last night and I am so glad that I experienced it. I reached the office and of course everyone was asking me if I was okay. I told them I was fine, but they didn't believe me. I wasn't sure how to explain what happened, but I do know that I felt like a new person.

As I sat at my desk, I begin to pray and ask God to strengthen me as I committed to work out my own soul salvation. I believe that God has something awesome in store for me and I also believe He was working some thing out of me.

CHAPTER EIGHT

Samaria couldn't have come at a better time. We prayed and read the word together each night. Precious would join us when she wasn't asleep. Not being judgmental, but God still had some work to do in my sister.

After Samaria and I finished praying, we got a cup of hot tea and sat and talked for a while. Out of the blue, the doorbell rang. Precious happened to be going into the kitchen at the time and she answered the door. I heard her laughing and then she directed whoever it was to the den. I put my mug down on the table and sat up on the edge of the sofa waiting to see who was coming. My mouth dropped open as Terry walked into the room. He was his normal self. "Hey baby", he yelled. He saw Samaria and said, "I apologize; I didn't know you had company." Quickly, I reacted by saying, "That's because you didn't call first Terry." I stood up and introduced Terry to Samaria and asked her to please excuse us.

Terry and I went outside and I let him have it. "Terry", I said. "How could you just stop by my house, without calling first?" He made me so angry because he stood there with a blank look on his face and his response wasn't any better. "You are my woman, so I should be able to come by anytime I want." I couldn't so anything but ask him to leave.

He told me he wanted to talk to Precious before he left. I told him I didn't think that was a good idea. He would have to leave and not ever come back to my house unannounced. He didn't like my demand too much and I really didn't care. I may have taken some things from Terry, but just dropping my house, isn't gonna work with me.

When I got back in the den, Samaria gave me a look that was more than odd. I knew I was in for it. "Passion", she said. "Please say it ain't so. Don't tell me that you're dating that guy again." I didn't know what to say, but I knew what not to say. So, I said, "You know Terry and I dated when we were in college, but we are just friends now. He has some things going on and said he wanted to talk to me about it. He and I are so long over and it was the best thing I could have done." In the back of my mind, I know I'm not over him. When I think I am, he shows up and I find myself wanting to be with him in more ways than one. He's the one person that could keep me from my destiny. I just couldn't understand myself for wanting to continue on in this counterfeit relationship. It's so sad that I know better, but I can't seem to walk away.

Samaria sits back in her chair and says, "This man is going to cause you some serious pain, if you don't cut him off in every way. You can't be friends with the devil, because he doesn't love you. He wants to use you and then leave you for dead. The devil's track record isn't good, but it is consistent. Get out Passion while you still can, it will be the second best decision you could ever make." She lets me know she's there if I need her to pray. I love my cousin dearly, and the truth is if she had not been there Terry still would be. Prayer is the only thing that is going to break this cycle with Terry in my life. I want to be free, but Terry is my best kept secret.

I have a lot to think about, because as quiet as it's kept, I have fallen for Kris. I believe he has stronger feelings for me to, but we have not said anything to one another. "Dear God, I need your help." I scream on the inside. This is the perfect time for me to relax in a nice warm bath, while I listen to some music that will minister to me. That is exactly what I did.

When I finished my bath and got dressed for bed, I went to make sure the doors were locked and that all of the lights were off. As I walked down the hall, it was quiet but I saw that the kitchen light was on. When I went into the kitchen, Precious was sitting at the table with her head in her hands. I immediately went into big sister mode. "Precious are you okay?" When I spoke, it startled her, because she had no idea I had even entered the room. She said, "I'm fine, nothing I want to talk about right now." I followed up with, "You sure?" Her response was low and slow, "I'm sure." I knew when she was ready to talk she would, so I just let it go.

I was about to walk away, but stopped and turned and asked, "Oh, by the way, what was it that Terry wanted with you?" She sat up with this "girl please", look on her face and said, "Nothing, you know Terry blah, blah, blah." I laughed and headed for bed. I yelled back down the hall, "Don't forget to turn the light out." When I passed the guest room, I heard Samaria going at it in prayer. When she's done someone is going to get a breakthrough for real. Little did I know it would be me.

I went to my bedroom and had a good talk with myself. I am so much better than I am acting. I don't even remember what caused me to get to this point, I'd love to retrace my steps and change some things and take myself out of this picture.

Samaria has me thinking, I certainly don't want my decisions to lead to my demise. I want the strength of God to help me over come this flesh driven connection.

After my self directed conversation, I read my bible, said my prayers and called it a night. I remember thinking, "God I need you to move in me" as I drifted off to sleep.

CHAPTER NINE

Today is Friday and I am only working a half day, because the function for Kris' parents is tomorrow night. I have some shopping to do. I also have to go to my hairdresser and get my hair done. After I am done there I will go to the spa for a facial, pedicure and manicure.

I pray these few hours go by fast, so that I can get underway. Samaria said she'd meet me at the mall to help me out. It's going to be a wonderful day.

My workday started out with a meeting, but it wasn't too long. We stuck to the agenda and the meeting was a success. I was glad because I didn't want anything to slow me down.

I was rushing down the hall to my office and Cheryl was trying to wave me down, I told her, "I can't stop right now, Cheryl." I was almost at my office, I told her to call me. I was in overdrive. I opened my office door, which I thought I left closed. I must be losing it. Oh, well I placed some papers on my desk, and turned around right into Terry's arms. It totally floored me. I figured out that Cheryl was trying to tell me, that someone was in my office.

After stepping into Terry's arms, he laid on awesome kiss on me. I didn't even fight him off. I'm ashamed to admit, that I liked it. All I could think was, "God please give me the strength to get this man off of me." Finally, that fine specimen let me go and stepped back. Ooooh, weeee this man is so fine. He smells so good and dresses like he just walked off of the pages of GQ magazine. He speaks, "Hey baby, you look wonderful." I just looked at him and said, "Terry, stop." All of a sudden I was back to myself. "Yes, stop", I said. "I can't go on like this with you anymore. You are in and out of my life and me like a fool will let you back in. Why? Because you're fine, you smell good and you dress nice. I am so stupid. There is no reason that I should allow anyone in my life that would cause me to sin. I am getting my life together and I refuse to sit in the pews of the church saying, "Amen" and then lay on my back with you and say, "Oh, baby." I want a relationship with Jesus Christ and I am going to have it. Since things are good between God and me, I believe He will give me a man after His own heart. Terry I am about Jesus now and not my flesh."

There was a little silence and then all of a sudden that joker broke out laughing. I couldn't believe it, he actually laughed in my face. Then he said, "Girl, you are addicted to me. We need to go on and be exclusive. I love God to and I know I can call on Him when I need Him and He will be there. You feel good to me and I know I feel good to you. That's reason enough for us to make this thing official. The church doesn't have to know what's going on, keep your business to yourself. I certainly won't be telling anybody." I was so angry. This man only sees me as an object and God as a genie or something. Only the spawn of satan could stand in your face and laugh after you've shared how you feel about God. I was ready to throw some blows. "Terry, you need to leave my office and leave now." I said. "Oh, baby, come on. You know me." "Yes, Terry I do know you and that's why I want you to leave." He says, "Okay, I'll go but just like Arnold Schwarzenegger, I'll be back."

I was furious as he walked out of my office. Just then the phone rang, it was Cheryl. "Passion, I was trying to tell you that someone was in your office." I interrupted and I said, "I figured that out once I got in here Cheryl. It's okay and I'm okay. Thanks for being concerned."

It was time for me to go. I said "Good-bye" to everyone and went to meet Samaria. I sure could use her prayers right about now.

I made it to the mall in one piece and headed to the entrance of Macy's, where Samaria and I planned to meet. As I walked up, she was sitting on a bench talking on her phone. When she saw me, she wrapped the conversation up by saying, "Mom, I'll call you later Passion is here now. I love you to." She looked at me and said, "Girl, I love my Mom, she is something else. She told me to tell her niece, she said "Hi". As she spoke I was off in la la land. "Hello, earth to Passion, are you there?" I snapped back shaking my head a little. "What?" I said. "Are you with me cuz?" "I'm here, just trying to get myself together." Samaria, leaned to one side and said, "Uh, oh what happened?" I didn't say anything right away, because I was wondering if I should tell her. I knew the only way I would be free, was to have someone to be accountable to. I gave Samaria a blow by blow account, of what had just happened at my office as we walked through Macy's. When I finished, I felt better and she said, "Girl, you better run and I mean run for your life. It sounds to me like the devil is trying to set you and keep you from what God really has for you. He's a counterfeit, that's why he could laugh so easily in your face. It's time to pray this brother away. You don't need any distractions. The enemy knows where you are going and he will do anything he can to keep you from getting there. I'm committed to praying until he is gone." I couldn't agree more with Samaria, but I was hoping it would work.

Terry needs to be out of my life, but there are times that I am just too weak to fight to be free. I am convinced now that God has sent Samaria to help me fight, not only that but to teach me how to fight in prayer.

69

We decided we'd talk about it later, right now I needed to find something to wear for tomorrow night and quick. I told Samaria about a great boutique, we found it and my hunt for a dress began. I knew I was only going to pick from five different dresses. It took us a minute, because I had to pick something that was easy to match shoes and accessories with. This boutique had everything a girl needed for a special affair.

I found a beautiful bronze colored dress, which means I don't even have to buy any shoes since I already own some bronze colored ones. Samaria thought the dress was a good choice. Even though she has a great relationship with Jesus Christ, she still has balance. She dresses nice, she loves to laugh and she loves to go to movies and do other recreational activities. I still have to say that if you ever need someone to pray for you, she's your girl.

I finished trying everything on, and I was pleased with my selections down to the accessories. Samaria and I grabbed a quick bite to eat and I left to go to the hairdresser. Samaria said she had to run a couple of errands and then she was going home. I told her, I would see her at the house later.

When I arrived at the hairdresser, there were about three ladies ahead of me. I spoke to everyone, sat down and begin to read my book. While I was reading, I began to think about my situation with

Terry and Kris. I am not sure if Kris feels the same for me as I do for him. I know the relationship between Terry and I, is all about the flesh. I can only ask God for His help in working this all out.

I know the obvious, but the obvious is not always easy to do. I fell in love with Terry while I was in college. He had a charm and wit about him that was second to none. Not to mention that he was extremely good looking. He swept me off of my feet and now that I think about it, he told me he'd be a part of me for the rest of my life. That statement was followed by, "Even if we aren't together." Almost scary, but I knew Terry would never do anything to hurt me.

Kris however, should be the man of every Christian woman's dreams. He loves God and is all about pleasing Him, and not his flesh. He's, a breath of fresh air.

I know it has only been a few months, but having him as a part of my life has been so refreshing. He's been nothing but a gentleman and very kind to me. He's an awesome man of God. He and his late wife had no children, so after she passed away he was by himself, until he went to his parents for a while. One thing, I admire about him is that he has not jumped into another relationship to soothe his pain. That would only make matters worse if the relationship did not work out. I came out of deep thought by Trina calling me. I knew I'd be done in about an hour once I sat down in *"the magic chair."*

CHAPTER TEN

It was 3:30pm and I was leaving the shop. As always Trina had me looking like I had just stepped off the page of a magazine. My eyebrows were arched and my up-do was tight, there was no way, that bad boy was moving. When she finished, I went into the back of the salon to get my manicure, pedicure and full body massage.

God had really blessed Trina. She went from having one salon to owning four full service salons, all in brand new buildings that she paid for with cash. She had a salon on each side of the city, that way her customers could go to the salon closet to their job or their home. She worked one day at each salon, but that wouldn't bother you because her staff was so good that you would feel comfortable with anyone of them. Yup, she was a blessed woman of God.

I was so relaxed; this was a much-needed pampering session. I knew of course, I couldn't be there without my telephone ringing. I answered only after looking at the caller ID and seeing that it was Samaria. "What's up cuz? I said. "Nothing much", was her reply and she continued.

"As I was driving to the house, I had the thought that you should get a gift and a card for Kris' parents. What do you think?" "I think you are a wonderful cousin, that's what I think. That is a great idea, and I will stop by Dillards on my way home. Thanks girl and I'll see you in a bit. " She said, "You're welcome" and we hung up.

My hands and feet were done, so I went to the dressing room put on my robe and headed for my table. I was excited and couldn't wait for them to start.

When I woke up, Ingrid was done. I felt like a new person. It was 6:30; I got dressed, paid my bill, made my next hair appointment and headed for Dillards. Since I didn't know, what Kris' parents liked a gift card was a great idea.

Once I was done at Dillard's, I stopped by Wal-Mart. I can't go into Wal-Mart without coming home with extra items added to my list. It's just awful no control in *"Wally World"*. I laughed to myself as I loaded the packages into my car.

All of a sudden I remembered, that we were having special prayer at church tonight. We had to write our prayer requests down on a piece of paper without our name, and drop them in the prayer box. When the

Lord answers the request, it is removed from the box by an intercessor. I called Samaria to remind her, and she was on her way.

I had a major request; I just had to find a way to word it. I needed to be delivered from my flesh. I can admit I want to be free from desiring Terry, but every time he comes around and touches me I just melt. I can't exactly write that on a prayer request, what would the intercessors say? I know, they don't talk they pray.

I don't think what I have done is cute, nor will I say I did not enjoy it. I can say I want to change, if I put it in the prayer box or not.

I made my way to the church, when I got there prayer was about to begin and much to my surprise Mr. Pittman was leading the service. He came before the congregation and shared a few words of encouragement with us. "Tonight we are here because so many of us have special needs we want to put before the Lord. Pastor has been encouraging us since the beginning of the year to totally trust God, to help us through our trials and situations. We often pray, but walk away from the altar looking back trying to figure out if God heard us. Trust me when I say, God heard you. If you are a sinner and you ask to be forgiven and for God to come into your heart, He will hear you. Tonight is another opportunity for us to take God at His word. Whenever you are ready, you can come up and bring your request on a piece of paper and drop it in the prayer box. Only God can do what we are asking Him to do, if we could have done it we would've done it a long time ago. If you haven't written your request yet we will give you some time to do so and remember no names. "

I went ahead and in a tasteful manner, I wrote out my request and put it in the prayer box on the altar. Once everyone was done, we all gathered around the altar and prayed corporately. While I was standing there praying, I pictured me with Terry. What in the world, I thought to myself. I promise I must have said "Dear Lord", about ten times. Okay, I tried again and this time I heard someone in my ear saying, "Push past the distractions and press in to God." I knew that voice was Samaria's. She stayed behind me and I was able to get a breakthrough in prayer. After praying corporately, we prayed individually and then Mr. Pittman closed or should I say "Assistant Pastor Pittman" closed the service and dismissed us.

I went to my seat to gather my things, after hugging a few of the members. Over the noise, I heard someone call out, "Passion". I was afraid to look up at first because I thought it was Terry, it wasn't though. It was my brother Paul. "Oh, my goodness Paul", I yelled out. "When did you get home?" He picked me up, swung me around and hugged me. "I just got here about two hours ago. I went by the house and Precious said you were here. It was good to see her, but I couldn't pick her up because she was too heavy. Besides she was so caught up in some gentleman caller. So, what's been up sis?", "Quite a bit has happened since you've been gone. I rededicated my life to Christ and I am now more active in the ministry. I've also met a nice guy that I have been hanging out with. I haven't told the family yet, because we are only friends." Of course Paul gives me this silly look. "It's about time ", he blurts out while smiling. We continued talking as we walked to the car. I followed him to our parents' house and that was a nice little ride.

When I drove up in the driveway, I promise it looked like every light in the house was on. Paul ran to my car and helped me out, still laughing at what I'd said earlier. He ran up on the porch, opened the door and said, "Announcing the Queen." My Mom and Dad said, "Boy what are you talking about?" I walked in the door and they both just about screamed. They were so shocked to see me. We live in the same city but I get so busy, that I don't visit like I should. We hugged one another and of course like most parents they said there is some food in the kitchen. I held my arms out like, do I look like I need to eat? Trust me my dress size doesn't say I'm lacking.

All of us sat around the kitchen table and laughed and talked. As I sat there, my mind went back to when we were all home and we sat at the table for breakfast and dinner. We talked about everything.

Mom and Dad were so good at listening to what we had to say about school and life. They knew when we did wrong and when the teacher did us wrong.

That kitchen looked the same. The color was a soft taupe, with the nice dark cabinets and beautiful granite counter tops. The paint blended so well with the granite. I remember sometimes I would sit in the kitchen with Mom and just talk while she cooked dinner. She is such a wise woman. I have always taken my Mom's advice, except when it came to Terry. That man was so intoxicating. I can imagine you may know that kind.

"You know we don't see you enough, Passion." "I know Dad; I promise I'll do better. I stay so busy with work and church." Paul interjects, "Don't forget your new friend." Mom looked at me and said, "A new friend?" I hope he's nothing like that Terry guy from your college days. There was something about him, that just didn't set well with your dad and I." I couldn't really say anything, but I attempted to. "Mom, he meant well. I've moved on and Terry and I haven't spoken in a while. I am in a new place and I trust God to help me make better choices, enough about Terry. Paul is home and we need to know what's up with him." Everyone agreed and the rest of the night was a blast. You have to know that the topic of the new friend did come back up, before the evening was over. I knew that it would get deeper before I left to.

I got up from the table and went into the kitchen for a slice of sweet potato pie. As far as I was concerned no one could make a sweet potato pie like Paul. I always ate my pie differently. I would warm it up, with some butter on top and a scoop of butter pecan ice cream on the side. That was some good eating.

While I was preparing my pie, Mom came into the kitchen. "So, Passion tell me about this new friend." I was a little nervous, because there wasn't really much to tell her. "Well, mom his name is Kris and he is a very nice man." I leaned my head to the side and said, "He's nothing like Terry", with a slight smile on my face. She lifted her hands as if she were praising God. "You don't have to worry about me Mom. Besides Kris and I are only friends and we are not talking about dating. We may go to lunch or dinner every now and again but that's it. I am going out with him tomorrow night, to an anniversary party for his parents. He asked me if I would be his guest and I said yes." She pulled out a chair and sat down; I knew this was now very serious. "Sit down baby", she said. I did. "Sweetheart, I know you are quite capable of taking care of yourself and making sound decisions. I am still your mother and one of the things I will always do is have concern about your well-being. I will also always want nothing but the best for you. Your father and I love you and we still pray for you every night, trusting God to keep you safe and in His will. I know you have grown to love God, but sometimes in our growing we are blindsided by the enemy and I want you to be in good defensive strength to fight that joker off."

The last thing I wanted my Mom to do was worry. I knew it wasn't much, but I got up from my seat and walked around the table and kissed her on the cheek and said, "Mom, I will be fine and you know God has got my back." She smiled and we were interrupted, by Dad and Paul coming into the kitchen. Dad, looked at Paul and said, "It appears some girl talk has been going on in here." I said, "Did we say anything about all that man talk and growling going on in the living room?" Dad just grabbed me and hugged me and said, "No baby, you didn't and you know it's okay if you did. I'm just glad to see you."

It was getting late and I had a nice long ride ahead of me, not to mention a long day tomorrow. Paul offered to drive me home in my car, and have Samaria bring him back tomorrow. He went up to his room, packed a duffle bag hugged mom and dad and we all said, "Good night".

When we got in the car Paul said, "Let's stop and get you some gas girl, you are almost on E." I told him he was driving do what he needed to do. Once we stopped and he filled up the car, we were underway. It would take us about an hour to get back to my house and I still had a few things I wanted to get done.

Paul relaxed in the drivers seat, looked at me and said, "Passion, I had no idea Mom and Dad would be so shocked about Kris. I guess I shouldn't have said anything. I apologize." "Paul, it's okay, you didn't do anything wrong. They would find out if Kris and I decide to get serious, so better now than later." We laughed. "You mind if I ask you about him?" Paul said. "No, I don't mind. As you already know his name is Kris. His Uncle is my boss, Mr. Pittman. He is a very nice man and more than anything he loves the Lord and has a strong relationship with Him." I could feel Paul looking at me, trying to get his thoughts together before he said anything. Finally, he speaks. "You sound like you really like this man, when do I get to meet him?" "I don't know maybe tomorrow", I said. "He invited me to his parents' 40th wedding anniversary celebration at their house." "Really?" Paul said. "That's almost like he's saying, he wants to get his parents opinion. It could be a big deal." In my mind I was thinking, Paul was going over board. I was only going to this event because we were friends.

Paul and I talked about some things going on in his life and listened to some new music I had. Paul really liked what I had purchased and decided he would pick up the same CD's before he left.

I called Precious to let her know, we would be home in about fifteen minutes. Paul was getting drowsy and I was trying to sing, talk, laugh and keep the windows down so that he would stay awake. We were both really tired.

We were about five minutes from the house, when this car hits us with its high beams and speeds up, flying past us. Once the car got closer, it kind of looked like Terry's car. Oh, well I'm sure there are plenty of black Jag's in the city. He wouldn't be over here anyway.

We made it to the house and I didn't waste any time saying *"good night"* and going on to bed. Paul and Precious started talking; I was surprised that she was even still awake.

I didn't realize how tired I was, until I laid down in my bed. I went to sleep almost immediately.

CHAPTER ELEVEN

I woke up later than I wanted to, it was 10:30am and 8:00am was my target time to get up. I had everything I needed for tonight, but I wanted to do some things around the house.

I got up, put on my robe and went to the kitchen. Paul was still asleep on the sofa and Precious was asleep in the recliner. That was a sight to see.

I got the coffee out of the pantry and brewed some. The smell of fresh brewing coffee always does me good. Since everyone was asleep I thought I'd wake em' up "Mama" style. I found my cast iron skillet, put it on the stove and put the eye on medium while I took the fresh thick cut country ham from the fridge, the kind with the bone in the center. I brought some a couple of days ago because I knew it would come in handy. The ham along with some cheese grits, eggs and homemade biscuits would certainly wake the house. You better know, as soon as I started that ham, there was some movement. Precious turning slightly in the chair, said "Mom is that you?" I laughed and said, "No, girl it's me. You need any help getting up off that chair? She just rolled her eyes at me.

Paul said, "If she does, I'll help her up." Can you believe what a little country cooking will do. I walked over to the living room only to see Samaria walking down the hall. "Is Auntie here?" I responded with, "Is my Mom the only person that can cook?" I was a little offended, by them asking if Mom was there. I can cook and they all need to recognize that. "Sis accept it as a compliment, because it sure does smell like Mom is in here." Paul said. I continued cooking and stirring the grits and scrambling the eggs with "love".

I set the table with Samaria's help and put the food in the center so we could all just serve ourselves, and no one would have to get up from the table to get anything. Home-style is always good, and the conversation keeps going. Paul blessed the food and it was silent until I finally said something. "Is everybody alright?" Paul replied with, "When you don't hear anything at the table when eating is going on, that means you put your foot in it." We all started laughing and Samaria chimed in, "Girl, I promise it feels like Auntie is here. You had to pay close attention to her when she cooked because this tastes just like her cooking". We all looked at one another for a few seconds and continued eating.

Once again the silence was broken, this time by Precious. "So, Passion, are you nervous about meeting Kris' parents tonight?" There was a hush at the table. I stumbled for words because I really hadn't talked about Kris much, especially to Precious. It seems like I would talk more to her being my sister, but for some reason we don't talk like that. Don't get me wrong though, we do a great relationship.

"What kind of question was that? Of course she's nervous" Samaria interjected. "Listen you guys, I know I haven't spoken to you all about Kris very much, but trust me when I say he's a wonderful man". I begin to smile and continued to speak. "When Kris and I met, I knew there was something very special about him. He was a gentleman and very respectful. He has yet to bring up the topic of sex and that is so very refreshing." "What?" No mention of sex. Run Passion run, that could only mean one thing, he's gay! Precious said with such confidence. "Precious, please just because he hasn't approached her like that doesn't mean he's gay." "Samaria is right", Paul said. "All men don't want to rush into sex and being that he is saved, that is not his focus." Precious sat on the edge of her seat and said, "So, what you are saying to me Paul is, that you don't step to women on the playa tip?" "We aren't talking about me Precious, okay."

I sensed tension rising between Precious and Paul, so I tried to redirect the conversation. "Listen you guys, all that matters is Kris has been nothing but a complete gentleman and I do have strong feelings for him. I have not said that to him, but he is a wonderful man and settling down with him would be an awesome blessing. I just don't always feel that I'm good enough for him."   Samaria chimes in with "Passion, please you are good enough for him, so stop tripping. You already know what God has for you is for you." No one ever really disagrees with Samaria, so I nodded and smiled. I got up from the table to take my plate to the sink and looked at the clock, I couldn't believe that it was 1:00pm. We had been talking for quite some time. Everyone helped me clean off the table and clean up the kitchen. Once the kitchen was done, I went back and took care of my bedroom and did a little laundry.

I begin to wonder what tonight would be like and I started to get nervous. What will Kris' parents think of me? More than that, why did Kris choose me to go with him? I have so many questions.

After I put my clothes in the dryer, I sat down to my computer to check my email. As usual, I had a ton of junk mail and I clicked empty. I scrolled through my inbox and deleted all the mail that was not important and read all the mail that was. I had emails from some friends, some co-workers, from the church and much to my surprise, an email from Kris. My mind began to race.   Was he canceling tonight?   Is something wrong? What could it be? The subject line had "About Tonight". I opened the email and began to read:

"Hi there Passion",

I am sending this email to you about tonight. As I told you my parents are celebrating their 40th wedding anniversary and this is important to our family. Anyone who means anything to us will be there. With that being said; Passion I've invited you out tonight because my feelings for you have grown into something very special. My heart beats constantly for you. I find myself waking from my sleep thinking about you and praying for you. I have shared my heart with God about longing to be closer to you and getting to know you better.

I felt I should share my feelings with you and let you know, that I am interested in taking this relationship to another level. I think you are a beautiful woman with a beautiful spirit to match and you accompanying me tonight means so much to me. Since the death of my wife, no other woman has come close to being interesting.

Thank you for being a part of tonight and for bringing me joy that I have not felt in a very long time."

Lovingly yours,

Kris

As I sat at the computer, my eyes began to fill with tears and they eventually ran down my face. While in my somber moment, Samaria knocks on my bedroom door. I couldn't say a word; I just got up and opened the door. She was yelling down the hall telling Paul to hurry up and get ready. After all of that, she turned to walk in the door and said, Okay, what happened? Why are you crying?" Again, I could not say one word, so I just pointed to the computer. Samaria sat down and began to read. When she finished, she got up and hugged me and said, "It sounds to me like the man of God has found his *"good thing"*. To think you felt you weren't good enough for him, nor his type." In that very moment, I realized more than ever that God is so in control. Going out with Kris tonight, now takes on a whole new meaning. I looked at Samaria and said, "I never knew Kris felt this way, should I change the way I act around him now?" "Of course not", she blurted out. "He was attracted to you, just like you are to him. Why in the world would you go and start doing something different? You are that brothers' *good thing*, I feel it in my bones." She was so well versed in the bible, I'll have to sit down with her later and talk about that verse. I think it's found in *Proverbs 18:22.* I may as well step back and let God do it.

Time is passing by so quickly and I have to get dressed. Tonight will be the first time; Kris comes to my house to pick me up. God give me peace and bless this night.

CHAPTER TWELVE

It is so funny, that tonight Precious, Paul and Samaria were all at the house with nothing to do until after I leave. They appeared to be more nervous than I was. Paul was pacing back and forth, like he was my father about to give his approval on my boyfriend.

I finished the final touches on my make-up, checked my hair, sprayed on my perfume, grabbed my purse and emerged from what was seemingly my dressing room. When I walked out into the hallway, the first person to see me was Paul. He stood there and his mouth dropped open. He was in total shock; you'd think I'd never dressed up before. As I continued down the hall, Samaria and Precious saw me and had the same reaction. Finally, Paul said, "Passion, you look absolutely stunning." "What?" I said. Precious chimes in, "Yeah, I have to totally agree with Paul, you look good!" I replied with, "Thank you". Then, Samaria speaks, "Passion, you are a vision of loveliness and you are going to cause that man to pass out. You make the scripture, *"we are fearfully and wonderfully made"*, come to life. Go on with your bad self". I smiled and right then the door bell rang, it was 6:30pm on the dot.

Samaria pushed me back down the hall, Precious sat in the recliner and Paul stood by the door with his hand on the door knob. Samaria ran to the guest room, grabbed a magazine and came back sat on the sofa, and nodded to Paul as if to say "action". Paul said, "Who is it?" The answer that came from the other side of the door was, "This is Kris". Paul opened the door and let Kris in. He reached out to shake his hand and said, "Hey man what's up? I'm Paul, Passion's brother. Good to meet you." Paul continued the introductions. This is our little sister Precious and this is our cousin Samaria. Kris reached out and shook their hands while responding with, "Nice to meet you all."

The three of them were smiling, well actually cheesing as they looked Kris up and down. Paul offered Kris a seat near the front door, so he couldn't look down the hall. Samaria said, "Excuse me, I'll go get Passion for you." I had gone into the den and was sitting on the sofa, praying my folks wouldn't ruin my night before it got started.

Samaria stuck her head in the door and asked, "Are you ready?" I got up straightened my dress out and walked into the living room. Kris, saw me, stood up, begin to grin from ear to ear and handed me a dozen red roses. He kissed me the cheek and told me, "Passion you look beautiful, thank you so much for accompanying me tonight." I told him thanks for the roses and for inviting me. Our eyes were locked on

91

one another the entire time. At that very moment, I felt so much love for him. Samaria took the roses from me and told me she'd put them up.

Kris took me by my hand; I almost passed out and he told everyone it was nice meeting them and goodnight. They told us goodnight and we left. As we walked to the car, I could feel them starring at us and I wanted to turn around and lick my tongue out at them so bad.

Kris opened the car door for me, as I got in I looked up and saw those clowns looking at us out of the window laughing and waving. I couldn't resist, before Kris got in I did lick my tongue at them. When Kris got in the car and started to back out, he flashed his headlights to signify he saw them. We both laughed and Kris said, "You have a nice family."

Kris' parents only lived about thirty minutes away, so we didn't have much time to talk. He did ask if I received his email. I told him that I did and I thought everything he wrote was sweet. He seemed to be relieved and said we'll talk more later.

We arrived at his parents' house where there were several cars in the driveway and on the street. All of sudden my nerves kicked in. When Kris got out of the car, I prayed a really quick prayer. He opened my door and helped me out, when I stood up we were face to face. He looked so handsome and at that moment all of a sudden out of nowhere, I pictured Terry's face. Oh, no I thought what is going on? I was quickly drawn from my thought, by Kris taking me by one hand with both of his saying, "Don't worry Passion, everything is going to be fine tonight." I smiled and we walked up the driveway to the house.

I didn't think anyone noticed we had walked into the house, because everyone was engaged in a conversation of some sort. Then all of a sudden I hear, "Passion, is that you?" I turn around and I'm amazed to be starring in the face of my boss, Mr. Pittman who looked quite jazzy and his wife, who is always beautiful. I smiled, and said "Yes, sir it's me". Mrs. Pittman gave me a hug and Mr. Pittman followed. They both complimented me on how I looked and Mrs. Pittman really loved my shoes and accessories. Kris asked me to excuse him and he'd be right back. Both he and Mr. Pittman walked away. I stayed right where I was talking to Mrs. Pittman, since I did not know anyone else.

The atmosphere was so pleasant and peaceful; you could feel love all around the room. Family members were chatting, as worship music played softly in the background. Everything was decorated so nicely; it looked like a page in a magazine.

Mrs. Pittman turned to say something to me and as she did, the lights flickered. They were bringing out the guest of honor. Mr. Pittman beckoned for Mrs.

Pittman to come and assist him. He escorted his sister, Mrs. Thompson and Mrs. Pittman escorted Mr. Thompson. Kris stood by me as his parents came out. Kris' cousin Kaitlin introduced them, it was like a wedding reception. The photographer was a familiar face, he takes pictures at all of our office functions and he was certainly doing a great job here tonight.

The room was quiet, as the Thompson's thanked everyone for coming out and helping them celebrate this milestone in God. They talked about how they had some hard times, but did everything they could within their power to live a drama free life. Mr. Thompson was adamant about not having drama and I don't believe he had any either.

After they greeted everyone, Kris' sister Daphne sang "Happy Anniversary", to the tune of "Happy Birthday". I thought Anita Baker was in the room. Her voice was sultry and rich, just made you want to chill. When she was done singing, she gave both of her parents a kiss on the cheek and she came over and gave Kris a big hug.

Daphne looked at me and said, "You must be Passion." I smiled and answered her with a quiet "yes". She continued. "I've heard nothing but great things about you. I know my brother and he is a good judge of character. He hasn't been this happy in a long time." I had tears welling up in my eyes. As I began to respond to Daphne, my phone started to vibrate. I know that family of mine couldn't possibly be calling me, knowing where I am. I quickly reached in my purse, pressed ignore and continued my conversation. "Daphne", I said. "Your brother has been nothing but a perfect gentleman, since we met. He's an amazing man and his love for God and his family is something that I will always cherish. I'm so grateful to God for allowing us to meet and start what I pray will be a life long friendship." Daphne responded, "God is so good and His timing is always right. Excuse me Passion, I'll be right back." Daphne went into the kitchen and just as she walked off my phone began to vibrate again. I figured it must be important, so I answered it without looking at the caller ID. "Hello, this is Passion and this better be important", I said. "It is baby, what's up?" Oh, my goodness it was Terry. I just hung up the phone and turned it off. He picked the worst time in his life to call me. I knew he would be upset, but I don't care I'll deal with that foolishness later. In the back of my mind, I was trying to figure out how I would deal with Terry. My mind was racing and I had no clue how to let him go.

"Passion, are you okay?" "What?", I asked as I turned around. It was Kris. "You okay?" "Oh, Kris I'm fine just zoned out for a moment. This is a wonderful party and everything is so nice." "Thanks, Passion. Come on over so you can meet my parents." I hesitated for a moment and he looked me in my eyes and said, "I told you everything was going to be fine tonight, so there is no need for you to be worried or afraid." Kris locked his fingers with mine as he walked me over to meet his parents. I was extremely nervous. "What if they don't like me?" I thought. Too late to think about all of that now we're right in front of them. Kris begins the introduction. "Mom, Dad I have someone I'd like for you to meet."

CHAPTER THIRTEEN

The moment of truth has arrived. Kris, finished his introduction, "This is Passion Taylor. Passion let me introduce you to my parents, Mr. Nathan Thompson and Mrs. Shirley Thompson." I extended my hand to Mr. Thompson and said, "Pleased to meet you." I did the same with Mrs. Thompson. I swallowed and waited. Kris' mom said, "Young lady, it is indeed a pleasure to finally meet you. My son speaks well of you all of the time. I know if he has good things to say you must be a wonderful person. Welcome to our home and I'm sure we'll be seeing more of you." "Thank you", I replied.

Mr. Thompson chimed in right after by saying; "Passion, our son has been a much happier man over the last few months, and we finally see why. It is always good when your children are happy and our son certainly deserves to be. It is our prayer that God will bless the two of you with a life long relationship. Thank you for coming and enjoy your evening." I followed with, "You're welcome and thank you for having for me."

Boy, was I glad that was over. Kris held my hand and we walked over to the fireplace. He asked if I was okay. I started to laugh and he knew what that meant. I took a seat in the chair next to the fireplace and Kris went over to speak to his parents. They talked for a few minutes, his mom hugged him and gave him a kiss and his dad hugged him and shook his hand.

Kris, Mr. and Mrs. Pittman and Daphne stood around his parents as the lights flickered again. Kris began to talk to the guest in the room. "Good evening everyone, I along with my family want to thank you all again for coming out to celebrate with my parents. This however, is not the only reason you are here." While Kris was speaking I couldn't help noticing how wonderful he looked. His medium brown skin; was smooth, blemish free, soft and had a unique glow. His eyes were a deep brown and pierced right through to my heart. His teeth were white and incredibly straight, braces I'm sure, but I don't care. He wore that tuxedo and crisp white shirt so well, he stood there clean cut and handsome. He was a well-put together man and I am so happy to be here with him.

I stopped daydreaming and got my bearings together. When I did, Kris was walking up to me while still talking. "As you came to celebrate my parents, you also came to celebrate me. Many of you knew my loving wife Melanie; she was a true gift from God. After three years of marriage, God took her to be his angel. I have lived a life of holiness ever since. I have received my healing and a release to move forward." He reached for my hand and I stood beside him. "I have also received the blessings of my family." My heart dropped to my feet, this can't be what I think. Kris continued, "Tonight I have to go on to the next chapter of my life." Kris turned to me and said, "Passion, the last few months of my life have been a blessing. Why? Because, I have you in my life. Ever since I met you, I knew you would be my wife." I begin to cry. "I pray for you everyday and night. I think about you all of the time and when we're apart, I only want to be with you more. My love you are my "*good thing*", and I want you in life forever." He took my hand and said, "I want to know if you will make me an even happier man and be my wife?"

The room was spinning, but I could see that everyone around me was smiling, clapping and some even crying. Kris wiped my tears away and looked into my eyes, with those deep dark brown eyes of his and said, "Be Mrs. Kris Thompson." I was trying to say "yes", but my mouth just wouldn't move. Finally, it came out, "Yes, Kris, yes!!" He kissed me on the cheek and after that, you could really hear clapping, cheering and crying.

Out of nowhere people started hugging me and saying, "Welcome to the family." Mr. Pittman said, "I hope this won't cause a conflict of interest at work." Talk about "LOL", he did. I had to sit down, because everything happened so fast. Kris sat down with me.

He said, "You weren't expecting this were you?" "Of course I wasn't", I said. Kris wore a smile of victory on his face, one that would say, "I did it, I pulled the wool over her eyes".

I started to cry again and Kris held me so tight. Oh, how I felt so safe in his arms. We talked a little and agreed to tell my family over dinner after church the next day. He said we could do it at his parents' house, since they were already in the celebrating mood. "My sister is a fantastic cook. You had a little taste tonight. She'll put a menu together, for a Sunday dinner and I am sure you will be happy." He seemed to be so confident that she would do a great job. I couldn't believe it; I am going to be married.

Daphne and Mrs. Pittman came out of the kitchen, each one of them carrying a cake. Daphne's said, "Happy Anniversary" and Mrs. Pittman's said, "Congratulations".

Kris' parents came over to us and said, "We pray that God will bless you with as many happy years, just as he has blessed us." Then they both looked at me smiled and said, "Welcome to the family." Kris asked his parents about having Sunday dinner there and they agreed. The night continued for another hour and we were last to leave, we said good night to everyone and Kris took me home.

While we were driving, Kris asked me if I was happy, I told him "yes". I said, "Kris you can't imagine how happy I am right now. I didn't think this would be happening to me, especially this soon and with you. "Why not?" Kris asked. "I don't know, I guess I feel like I don't deserve it. I am however, grateful that it did." He sweetly said, "Me too." For the remainder of the ride we decided that I wouldn't tell anyone at the house, we'd tell my family tomorrow at dinner. Not saying anything was going to be so hard for me, so Kris kept the ring that way I wouldn't be tempted to put it on and show it off.

We got to my house around midnight. Kris turned the headlights off before turning into the driveway, that way the crew wouldn't know we were there yet. We sat in the car for another 30 minutes and talked about our engagement. I was still in shock, excited but in shock. Kris did say he didn't want a long engagement and I thought that was good. What he did say; put me in deeper shock. "Passion, like I said I don't want a long engagement. I would love to walk down the isle in about two months." "Two months", I said. "Does that bother you?" "No, Kris it doesn't, I just have to say I was not expecting that answer." I understood Kris' take on it, when you know it's God why prolong things. This would have to be God, because I will need him to plan this wedding in two months.

Kris discussed taking me to look at two houses he was in the market for buying, but he wanted to include me in on the decision. We would be looking at those houses on Monday.

His house was paid for and we agreed to pay my house off after the wedding. We would let family members occupy the houses and pay us a meager amount in rent.

Kris walked me to the door, kissed me on the cheek and said, "Passion, thank you for such a lovely evening. I love you and I'll see you in the morning." "No, Kris thank you for a lovely evening, just pray that I can keep my mouth closed." He waited until I unlocked the door and walked in. What a sweet ending to a wonderful night. Now, for one thousand questions from the crew.

CHAPTER FOURTEEN

The sun was beaming through my bedroom blinds and Paul, Samaria and Precious were all in my face. "Good morning Sunshine", Precious yelled out. "How was your date last night?" she added. I hadn't really opened my eyes; I hadn't brushed my teeth and I wasn't ready to talk about last night.

I sat up and managed to get a word in between the rumblings of Precious. "If you all must know, last night was fantastic. We had a wonderful time and Kris' parents are great and his family is awesome." "So, did you hit it big with the parents?" Paul asked. "Hit it big?" I said. "Yeah, Passion you know what I mean. Did they like you?" "I think they did Paul; as a matter of fact they invited all of us over for dinner after church today." "What?"! Samaria shouted. "Sounds like, they may like their sons "good thing". I had to reel them in real quick, before I spilled the beans. "Okay, everybody calm down. We are going over to his parents' house today to have dinner, fun and fellowship. When you get over there, why don't you ask Kris some of the questions you're asking me?" Paul said, "Don't worry I'm going to ask that young man a few things, watch me."

I quickly got off the subject and suggested breakfast. They were all down with that and even volunteered to help a sister out. Samaria was nominated to cook. While she cooked we all took our showers and got dressed for church. Samaria would take her shower while we prepared our plates and started eating.

I was in the mirror about to put on my make-up; I looked at myself and begin to thank God for blessing me. Immediately the tears started flowing. At that point Samaria called us to eat. I didn't move right away, I had to get me together.

The house reeked of bacon, but that wasn't all she cooked. They talked about my cooking being good, but Samaria was a far better cook than me. Everyone came out all dressed and ready to throw down. Samaria made all the plates and we could just bless the food and eat. Paul however, didn't want to pray and we knew Precious wasn't going to pray so I did the honors.

Once we started eating my cell phone rang, I jumped up from the table and ran to answer it. Kris was probably calling to see how my night went. "Good morning", I chimed and all I heard was, "So, now you're answering your phone." It wasn't Kris. "Terry, first of all good morning and second, what is your problem?" "You know what the problem is Passion, you hung up on me last night." I had to remain calm. "Terry, listen I apologize for hanging up last night. I was at an important function and I couldn't talk." Terry cleared his throat and said, "Passion, nothing should ever be more important than your man." I know he is not still trying to lay claim to me. "Terry look, I don't have time to go through this with you because I am trying to get ready for church. I will give you a call later on this evening." I hung up and went back to the table.

"Mr. Right called to say good morning?" "Okay, Paul you got jokes. That's good, but it wasn't Kris. After saying that I looked at the clock, it was 9 o'clock and church starts at 10:45. "Look at the time", I shouted. "We've got to get out of here in thirty minutes, in order to get to church in enough time to get a good parking spot." I left the slow pokes at the table and finished my make- up and hair. I put my shoes on and I was ready to go. I couldn't help thinking about Terry's call though. I really need to get a few things straight with him and help him on his way.

We all rode to church in my car and Paul said he'd drive. Our parents were going to meet us there and we all planned on sitting together during the service. I was really ready for this day to be over, because I was about to explode.

We got to church and found a great parking space and Kris and his parents pulled up right beside us.

We got out of the car, greeted one another and walked into the church. My parents were standing in the lobby when we walked in. I made all of the introductions, everyone said good morning and we started to walk into the sanctuary. My mom however, stopped with a questioning look on her face. That look, then became a surprised look. My mom turned to Kris' mom and said, "Shirley, Shirley Anderson?" Mrs. Thompson stopped, looked at my mom and said, "Yes, it's Thompson now." My mom continued, "Shirley, it's me Mildred, Mildred Davis from Highland Park High School." Mrs. Thompson was shocked and replied with, "What?" "Oh, my goodness Mildred how have you been?" "I have been doing fine Shirley, blessed with a beautiful family and grateful that all of my kids have been a blessing. I can't believe it's you, I somewhat thought it looked like you when Passion introduced us but I didn't want to stare." Kris' mom was just as excited as my mom was, she told my mom they would catch up at dinner.

The crew and I looked at one another and we were all surprised that our moms went to school together. Go figure what are the chances of that happening. Kris put his arm around me and squeezed my waist, indicating that he was happy that our moms knew each other.

Once entering the sanctuary we were all able to sit together. As soon as we sat down, Minister Faber came up to open the service. He greeted the congregation, read a passage of scripture and began to exhort. He gave the microphone to the Praise and Worship leader and service was on.

I have always admired my Pastor, Pastor Mark Gresham. He's a powerful man of God; he stands tall in the natural, but even taller in the spirit. His reputation precedes him. He's a man of prayer, faith and integrity. He walks in the office of a Prophet and when he speaks something, you better know it's going to come to pass. The people that I know, that he has spoken a word to said, "The word he spoke to me came as a confirmation to something God had already said to me in prayer."

Pastor Gresham loves God and the people of God. He constantly encourages us, to seek the will of the God for our lives. I can honestly say that God has used him, to help me to get where I am today. Since I've been a member of "Love Abides Family Life Center", I have learned the true meaning of having a real relationship with Jesus Christ. Not only that, but I have learned how to apply the word of God to everyday situations and I've actually seen the word come alive in my life.

I remember once when I first rededicated my life to Christ that the word came alive through healing. The scripture says: "The effectual fervent prayer of the righteous man availeth much." I had to stand on that and trust God to heal my body and He did.

CHAPTER FIFTEEN

Today's service was awesome and the power of God moved mightily. I know the entire congregation had to get something from the message. If they didn't then they just weren't tuned in.

After the benediction we all greeted various people in the congregation and met up in the foyer. The riding arrangements changed, Kris' parents rode with my parents, I rode with Kris and Paul still drove my car with Samaria and Precious. Everyone fell in line behind us and we were on our way to dinner.

Once we started driving, Kris reached over and took my hand and said, "I love you Passion." Chills ran down my spine when he said that and that had never happened before. I looked over at him and said, "I love you to." We were both a little more at ease about telling my family we're getting married; since we found out our moms know one another. How funny is that? Daphne left service a little early so that everything would be done, and we could all walk right in and eat. Some of Kris' cousins met her to help her out.

We pulled up in the driveway, Kris said a quick prayer and squeezed my hand. We got out of the car and waited for everyone to walk up the driveway. My sister was carrying on as usual, talking about "Girl, they have a lot of land, if you marry Kris you may be marrying into money." She laughed all by herself.

When we walked in the house, it reeked of good cooking. You could smell collard greens, candied yams, fried chicken, black-eyed peas and Mac – n-cheese. The aroma was so strong; it felt as if you had already eaten some.

The table was already set, with food in place. All we had to do, was wash our hands and take a seat. We did wash our hands, but we sat around and talked for a few minutes we didn't want to look like we were hungry.

Daphne asked me if I would give her a hand, so I went into the kitchen with her. Once in there, she said, "You look a little nervous, so I thought I'd bring you in here for a little breather. I told her "Thanks". She showed me the cake she ordered and picked up on the way home; I must admit it was absolutely beautiful. It was a sheet cake with purple writing and yellow roses. Not to mention butter cream icing. I could hear everyone laughing and having a good time out in the family room.

Daphne was busy putting the finishing touches on everything, when all of a sudden she stopped and stood over the sink. I walked over to her and asked if she was okay. She in turn took a deep breath and said, "Passion, I love my brother and one of the hardest things was to see him go through the loss of Melanie. He deserves a good life and certainly a good woman to walk beside him. Please take good care of him, but most of all love him with your whole heart and don't hurt him." I most certainly was not expecting that. Daphne didn't give me a chance to respond she just picked up a tray of food and walked out of the kitchen with it. When she returned, she smiled and said "Girl, it's time to eat. Let's take the rest of this food out to the table." I smiled and was relieved. As we both walked out of the kitchen, everyone started clapping and cheering as if they had been waiting for hours. We left the cake in the kitchen; Daphne would bring it out later.

Mr. Thompson called us all around the table, we joined hands and he blessed the meal, prayed for both families and the good fellowship. At the end of the prayer all of the men in the room let out a resounding "Amen!"

Kris and I sat beside one another, as did all of the married couples that were present. Other friends and family members were there that knew about the engagement and of course some were there that didn't know.

I was so extremely nervous and I could not just sit there, so I helped Daphne clear the table. When I went into the kitchen, Daphne said, "You should be at the table because I'm about to bring the cake out." I swallowed hard and asked, "Are you sure, you don't need any help in here?" Daphne looked at me as if to say, "Girl, get out of this kitchen." I didn't say anything else, I just walked out.

Daphne came out and announced the desserts. She said, "We have, sweet potato pie; 7-up cake; peach cobbler; German chocolate cake; red velvet cake and ice cream.

After Daphne finished that mouth-watering list, everyone suggested she bring them all out, so, she did. Paul was not shy about cutting into the red velvet cake and when he did it started a chain reaction. Once we all begin to dig in, Daphne came back out with the celebration cake and stood next to Kris. Precious looked up and said, "More cake? You all must have a bakery out back." Everyone started to laugh. By this time Kris was standing up with his hands in his pockets. He looked wonderful. He was wearing a gray suite with a lavender shirt. It was accented with a gray, lavender and white tie and matching handkerchief. His shoes were black loafers and they had a shine that made them look brand new.

Kris cleared his throat and said, "Excuse me." The chatter in the room stopped and everyone looked up at him as he stood at the dining room table. "I would like to thank you all for coming to dinner today, my family and I are truly grateful. Your coming out today was not only for dinner, but for some exciting news as well. I have prayed, talked to my parents and my uncle about my decision and now I want to share it with you." I was sitting in my seat and I had no idea how he was going to do this. I sat in that seat rocking back and forth like Sophia from the "Color Purple". Kris took me by hand and stood me up. I looked around the room as discreetly as I could, when I did I caught Samaria's eye. She nodded at me and smiled. I saw my Mom wiping tears from her eyes and it was at that moment that my eyes begin to fill with tears.

Kris continued, "I am so glad to say that I have asked Passion to be my wife. After spending time with her and knowing that God has given me the go ahead, I am honored to share the rest of my life with her. More than that, I am so glad that she said yes!" You could hear sighs all around the room and the tears begin to roll down my face. Kris took my hand and placed the ring on my finger. Kris' mom was crying and believe it or not, Precious was laying on Paul's shoulder crying.

113

Everyone applauded and lined up to hug us. While they were lining up, Kris made another announcement. "I forgot to mention, that we will not have a long engagement. We plan to be married in two months. I know Passion is the woman God has given me to be my wife and I don't need to wait any longer. So keep us in your prayers as we begin to plan. " I really begin to cry then. I noticed our parents were off to the side talking. I know my parents were elated; especially my Mom since she and Kris' Mom were friends in high school.

I can't believe how God has blessed me, even with all that has been going on secretly within me, God still saw fit to give me a man that loves Him and adores me. I don't want to break God's heart or Kris' heart, in order not to do so I have to talk to Terry. Wait, I don't have to tell him anything, I can just move on with my life and eventually he will get the picture. If he doesn't it isn't my fault, it's his own. I zoned back in on the festivities and I was happy.

Several friends and family members were there including some of my co-workers. I looked across the room and saw Cheryl and Peggy. They both came running over to me laughing. "Congratulations!" Peggy said. "I want to see the ring", Cheryl blurted out. So like her. "Wow, looks like he spared no expense," she added.

The both of them were genuinely happy for me and I

appreciated them for that. I had to ask Peggy one question. "Peggy", I said. She answered, "Yes". I need to ask you something and she said go ahead. "Was everything alright, when you were in Mr. Pittman's office on Thursday?" Peggy smiled and answered in her soft way. "Yes, everything was fine; we were actually meeting about this weekend. Mr. Pittman felt we should be here. I called and ordered the cake. I also called and told Cheryl after work on Friday, she's a great person but some things can't be discussed with her too early." I agreed.

We were all having such a good time that we didn't realize how late it was. As the guest begin to leave, Daphne, Peggy and Cheryl begin to clean up. Daphne was urging Precious and Paul to take some food home with them; she didn't want to have to find space in the fridge for all of that food. Paul was all over the offer. Daphne was laughing, as he stood in front of her 6'3" tall weighing 260 pounds. She didn't have to guess if he could eat what he was taking, because she was sure he could.

CHAPTER SIXTEEN

After all of the clean up was done, everyone left except Kris myself and our parents. We all sat down and talked. Mr. Thompson began by addressing Kris. "Son, we know this is a very big step for you and you've been praying about it for a few months. Your mother and I want you to know, you have our support, love and our prayers. We are more than confident that you will make a great husband and one day a wonderful father." Kris stood up and hugged both of his parents.

After hugging his parents, he turned around and addressed my parents. "Mr. and Mrs. Taylor, I want to first thank God for blessing you all with such a beautiful daughter. Secondly, I want you to know that I will take very good care of Passion. The order of my life will be; God, family, church and my career. I love your daughter and with God being the head, I will provide for my family. It is my desire for us to grow old together and walk in the will of God." Kris turned to me. "Passion, you know my story about my first wife. I didn't think that I would find another woman that would capture my heart. You have and I am so very happy. You are more than what I prayed for. It is as if God opened the door to my heart, walked in and evaluated my every desire for a wife.

Every since we bumped into one another in the hallway, I knew you were the one for me. After that incident, I begin praying for you daily and then I subtly expressed my interest. You're a woman of integrity, you're beautiful, you're caring, you're honest, you're loving and a true woman of God. I love you and I am excited about spending the rest of my life with you. I know you were shocked, when I said I didn't want a long engagement. I thought to myself, why should it be long when I love you. So, with that being said, I'd like to know if you'll agree to set our wedding date for June 23rd?"

I was so happy that he went ahead and set the date. "Kris", I said. "You really were serious about not having a long engagement; I think a year is perfect for planning." He smiled and said, "No, Passion not next year, still two months from now." I was hoping he had forgotten about the two months. I guess not. That short engagement stands firm." He looked at me and asked if that was okay, I responded with a "Yes"! It was settled the wedding was on for Saturday, June 23rd and we were both excited. In the words of Pastor Gresham, "When God moves, He sometimes moves really fast."

"Kris, I am honored that you have chosen me to be your wife. It is my prayer that I will be the wife you deserve." In the back of my mind, I was thinking about the fact that I was still connected to Terri. I

117

know that it has to end tonight. If I call him, it will only make it harder to let go. I will deal with that later, but right now I have a wedding to plan. As I come back to reality, I hear Kris saying, "I believe you will be." He extends his arms and we hug.

I looked at my parents and my Dad was holding my Mom, as she lay on his shoulder crying. I walked over to the sofa and sat down beside them. I put my arms around them for a group hug and I begin to cry with my Mom, my Dad managed to hold it together. Mom looked at me and said, "Sweetheart, God has really blessed you with a kind God fearing man. I know it appears that things are moving so fast, but God knows best. He had this all divinely planned from the beginning of time. I will continue to pray for you and I know you will be a great wife." I couldn't help but cry after that.

Kris and I walked out on the porch, while our parents said their good-byes. It was a beautiful night and I was with a handsome man, my man. We sat down on the swing and looked at the stars. Kris put his arm around me, but that was it. I of course am use to more, but he is a gentleman and respects me. Kris finally broke the silence. "Mrs. Passion Thompson, I like the sound of that. You would not believe how many times I have said that at home, alone." "I can imagine", I responded with a smile on my face. "I am so glad, that we don't have to change our church?" I said. Kris was glad about that to.

As we sat there under the stars, I was thinking about what it was going to be like being a married woman. Being with such an awesome man, all of the time and eventually having his children. I know I could never take the place of his first wife, but I pray I am everything he desires me to be. I turned to say something to Kris, and he was fast asleep on my shoulder. About the same time our parents came out. I gently kissed him on his forehead and he woke up, stretched looked at me and said, "I'm comfortable in your arms already." That really made me smile.

Well, we said our good nights to our parents and Kris took me home. We chatted a little on the way to the house, but mostly we held hands and just felt a great peace about our new life we were about to start together.

"Sweetheart, I am going over to the house tomorrow and check things out. I want to make sure nothing else needs to be done. I know we want the sitting room expanded in the master bedroom and the fence put up around the property. Can you think of anything else?" I sat and thought for a moment and it struck me. "What about the closet, are we going to have them re-do it? We need so much more space in there and I would love to have the drawers and the island in the middle." "Okay", he said "I'll make sure to mention it to the contractor.

Wow, I wonder if it will always be that easy. I know better. We will certainly have some disagreements, but we will be able to work through them.

We reached my house and the ride seemed shorter than usual, I really didn't want to leave Kris tonight but I had to go to my own house. We said good night to one another and he gave me a gentle kiss on the cheek. Boy, I'll be glad when these days are over and he can really say good night.

I was so surprised to see that most of the lights were out in the house; I guess everyone was too tired to wait up for me. As I walked to the front door I turned and waved good night to Kris, he smiled and waved back. He is such a sweet man and I am going to love being married to him.

I locked the front door and when I walked down the hall to go to my bedroom, everyone came out of the den. The scared me stiff. Of course they were all laughing and staring me up and down.

"What's up, oh great engaged one?" Precious said. I looked at her and said, "You are so, silly girl." "Silly, but I am loving the new stage in my sister's life. Paul chimed in with an "Amen". I knew they weren't going to go anywhere soon, so I figured I might as well give them some time and talk about the day's events.

"Listen, you guys Kris and I did go ahead and set our date for the wedding." "Yes, Lord it's official." Samaria managed to say, without doing a praise dance. I couldn't help but smile. I continued. Now, I don't want anyone to get too excited, but Kris and I will be getting married in two months, on June 23rd." "WHAT?" they all said at the same time. "You all heard me." "Wow, Kris is really serious isn't he?" Paul asked. "Yes, he is quite the serious one", I said.

As the crew continued to speak in the background, I begin to allow things to run through my mind. Here I am in the prime of my life, about to marry an awesome "Man of God". My family is excited, the groom is excited and me, well, I am excited but my mind is so clouded. I still have the issue with Terri. It can be solved with one phone call and why I keep avoiding it, I don't know.

CHAPTER SEVENTEEN

I made it through the night and all of the questions from my family. We finally went to bed around 3:00am and I had to get up early for work.

The alarm went off and I jumped up out of the bed and into the shower. I don' think I have ever gotten dressed so fast. No time for coffee or anything, I'll grab some at the office. It is 7:15 and I have to be to work at 8:00, traffic will be crazy and I'll be pushing it. Lord, let the traffic flow nicely.

Before I knew it, I was at the office and greeted with a great big smile from "Cheryl". "Good morning, Ms. Taylor". I couldn't resist smiling and saying "Good morning", right back at her. I walked down the hall towards my office, when Mr. Pittman (he's still my boss) beckoned me to his office.

"Good morning, Passion", he started. "Good morning, sir". He began, "I called you in this morning to tell you that I am going to let you take an early vacation. I know you have a wedding to plan and that all has to be done in about eight weeks. You are a wonderful assistant and I want to keep you. I will however, not allow you to run yourself ragged. So, starting today you are officially on vacation. No need to worry, all of our clients are well aware of your time off and we will be fine until the 1st of August."

I have to admit, I loved this offer and I'm going to jump on it fast. I replied "Mr. Pittman, thank you so much for this. It means more to me than you'll ever know. I have so much to get done and I was actually wondering when I would have the time. Now, I don't have to worry. I appreciate your thoughtfulness." He smiled and said, "Well, you better get going. When I get to that wedding I want to see a happy beautiful bride and a happy handsome groom." We hugged and I left his office. I couldn't leave the building, without going by my office and looking at a few things. I tidied up a bit, said my see ya - laters and went by the house to pick up Samaria. I'm excited, that we can get some shopping done.

I pulled up in the driveway and rushed in the house. When I walked in, I heard Samaria praying and she was putting it down. She was covering everything from the government to our family. I have always admired her prayer life and I am working my way towards a stronger one.

I went into my room to change my clothes. As soon as I finished dressing, Samaria came into the room sobbing really hard. I took her by her hand and asked her what was wrong. She managed to pull herself together and tell me to sit down. I did. What she said after I sat down almost blew me away.

"Passion", she started. "I have to be obedient to God, you know I take my prayer time very serious and when God tells me to tell someone something, no matter who it is I have to do it. As I was praying today, the Lord led me to tell you this: "If you don't stop your association with Terry, it will cause disaster. I have blessed you with a man that loves me and will love you as well. Terry is not the man I have chosen for you and it is time to be bold and end it." My mouth was open. Samaria said what she had to say and went back into her room and wept.

My body begins to tremble and the tears begin to fall. I knew it was God. I had put this off for too long and I know it has to happen. Now, God was saying "just do it". Not only was God saying to cut off the association, He meant it. No one knew about the relationship but Samaria and I knew she wouldn't tell anyone. I need God's strength to do this. I fell to my knees and begin to weep; I had no words just tears.

After about 15 minutes, Samaria came back into my room. She climbed up on my bed, laid down beside me and begins to pray. I start crying again, because her prayer seems to touch my heart so deeply. I know that Terry has been a downfall for me and I can't allow him and the lustful desire I have for him to continue to drive me. Staying away won't solve it, but cutting him off will. I have to do this, because if I don't Terry will continue to pursue me. I have a decision to make.

Samaria will do what God says even if it hurts the other persons' feeling. She hasn't always done that because she was afraid to. It was all up to me obey God. I never in my life ever imagined I would be found in this place.

Once Samaria and I pulled ourselves together, I filled her in on what had happened at work and wanted her to go with me and my Mom to pick out my wedding gown and help me with a few other things. After what just happened, this would have to be done tomorrow morning.

We didn't talk anymore for the rest of the day about what happened. Trust me when I say it was in the back of mind.

CHAPTER EIGHTEEN

Not having to get up and go to work was going to have to take some getting use to. I don't know how to sleep late, but I think I could learn. After having a nice long dinner with my family and resting well, I was ready to get on with the wedding plans.

I gave Kris a call and we chatted for a few minutes. He already knew about his Uncle giving me the time off, to get the wedding plans under way. I am so excited because we are going to look for flowers, talk to the caterer (who happens to be friends with Kris' family), pick paper for the invitations, napkins, place cards and thank you cards. The day I have dreamed of for so long, is finally here and I feel so undeserving. God is truly amazing.

I got dressed and Samaria and I had breakfast and we were off by 8:30 am catching the places that opened at 9:00 am first. We were successful in finding the colors I wanted, pink and brown. The invitations are adorable, yet elegant and the favors are sweet, literally. It is 12 noon, Samaria and I are going to pick up my Mom, have lunch and off to the bridal store. I made up my mind already on the design and I will be wearing ivory, Kris and I discussed it and he is okay with my decision. He is such a supportive man. I mean, why wear white when I know the truth and besides, it's best not to pretend.

We picked my Mom up and went to Lenoche' Grill. They have the best nachos, salads, sandwiches and desserts. Mom was excited about being with us for this fun filled adventure. Mom talked to Samaria a little about how things were going for her. You know Mom was in for an ear full.

Once we finished our lunch we went across the street to the Bridal Boutique. Before we went in, Mom told me to only look at three gowns because after that they all start to look the same. I already had a design in mind, I was going to make sure I looked for that style and that style only.

The young lady that assisted us at Marsha's Bridal Boutique was really sweet, her name was Brittany and she was willing to help me stay focused. I was falling in love with each gown I tried on, they were all so lovely. "Mom", I asked, "What about this one?" It was ivory, with Australian crystals all over the bodice; it was slightly off the shoulders, a low back, form fitting in the waist and wide at the bottom like a ball gown. The train was about 3 feet in length and the veil once flipped back, went down to the back of my knees. It was absolutely beautiful. I think I have found my wedding gown. Samaria thought it was the dream gown. I'm excited. "God thank you for an amazing day and for pointing me in the right direction, for all of the things I needed today. Amen."

As we drove back to my mom's house, my mom looked over at me and said, "I am so happy for you Passion and I pray that God will bless your marriage, as He has blessed your father and I. You have always been such a good girl and I want the best for you." I smiled as my eyes began to well up with tears and said, "Mom, I know God will bless us, just make sure you stay close by in case I need you for some pointers." We both looked at one another and I knew from the way she nodded, that she would be there any time I called.

After we dropped Mom off, we headed for home and decided on the way that we would bake some chocolate chip cookies; have some milk and address some invitations. Samaria was determined she would help me and host my bridal shower. Precious would help as much as she could, when she could.

Samaria and I went into the house and changed our clothes. Shortly after we got there, Precious came home. "Hey peeps, what's up?" She said after she walked in. "Nothing much?", Samaria responded. I laughed, because it was always funny listening to Samaria try and talk slang. "We are about to make some chocolate chip cookies; eat them and drink some milk. When we are done we are going to address some invitations. You want to join us?" I asked. She quickly said, "Yes, I am always down for some good eats. Let me change my clothes and I'll be right out." Samaria and I looked at one another and shook our heads.

This was going to be so much fun, we hadn't done anything like this in a while. Precious changed her clothes quicker than I had ever seen. She came into the dining room and sat down with us. We got everything we needed and the fun began. I mixed the dough, Samaria put the dough on the cookie sheet and Precious put them in the oven. After a while we had some hot fresh cookies. We ate cookies and laughed and talked. We reminisced about our childhood and teen days, we were something else.

I went into the den and got the bag with the invitations in it. I looked over on the table and saw that I had two missed calls. I picked it up and saw that one call was from Kris and the other call was from Terry. My heart started racing, my face became hot and I felt faint.

I texted Kris, turned the phone off, put it down and went back into the living room to address the invitations. Samaria was laughing so hard, when I got back in there, that I thought she was going to go into hysterics. "What's so funny?", I asked. She managed to stop long enough to share a moment she remembered about Precious when we were younger. I just happened to remember what she was talking about and couldn't help but laugh myself. I quickly forgot about Terry.

We addressed all of the invitations and placed the stamps on them. Precious asked, "So, where is the dress?" I want to see it. I without hesitation, grabbed her by the hand and took her into my bedroom to see it. When I pulled it out, you could have heard her scream for miles. I had to make sure she didn't jump up and down. "This is so gorgeous, you picked well sis. I may barrow this one instead of buying one when I get ready to tie the knot." I looked at her with a smile on my face and said, "When it's your time to get married, you'll want your own gown not a used one from your sister." She thought for a moment and said, "Yeah, you may be right."

As I sat there talking to them, I some what drifted off. I begin to think about what Terry could possibly want. It has been a while since we have spoken to one another and I know when we talk it is going to be flamed filled.

Terry is serious about having me to himself and it isn't going to set well with him that I am going to get married. I can say that finally I will be over Terry because I'll be happily married.

"Passion, Passion snap out of it." I heard Precious say. I don't know how long she'd been calling my name. "Yes", I said in a startled tone. "You must have really been in deep thought girl", Precious said. "What's up?" I had to think of something really quick so I said, "I was thinking about the wedding. I am so excited and nervous at the same time." "You aren't getting cold feet are you?" Precious asked. I looked and said, "Of course not!" "I hope not girl", Samaria said. "We are working too hard on these invitations and too many people are coming to town for this blessed event. So, you might want to pull it together." I took a deep breath and said, "Don't worry, I have it all together."

CHAPTER NINETEEN

Time certainly has gone by since we begin to plan the wedding. I am two days away from walking down the isle, and becoming Mrs. Kristopher Thompson.

My family has already started coming into town and Kris and I have had very little time alone. We knew that would be the case, but we are grateful for the time we have had and the lifetime we will have.

Tomorrow night's rehearsal and dinner will be so beautiful. The menu will consist of barbecued chicken and ribs, baked macaroni and cheese, sweet potato soufflé, corn on the cob, garden salad, broccoli and assorted drinks. Kris and I are going to give gifts to our parents and of course gifts to our wedding party.

We are having the reception at our church. The dining hall will be decorated, by a friend of ours and she will do the catering as well. We are having a full course dinner that will include; French onion soup or cream of broccoli soup, baked chicken and lamb, mashed potatoes, fresh green beans with thinly sliced red onions, rolls, ceaser salad and iced tea. The dessert of course will be the wedding cake. It is five tiers of sheer Red Velvet heaven, with cream cheese icing and pecans on the side in small cups. The cake was made by an award winning baker, "Booker the Baker" to be exact. He put a spin on the icing that is sure to please. Each layer is a gift box varying in size, each one a little larger than the other. They each have a red ribbon tied around them, trimmed in silver. Intricate lace designs on each layer. It's simply beautiful.

Not only is Mr. Booker an excellent baker, but he is married to the beautiful actress Naomi Lavette. She is so nice and if you ever want to laugh, go see her in one of her productions. You won't regret it.

The cake he designed for Kris is in the shape of a cross. It's a lemon cake with deep yellow and gold butter cream icing. The gold icing was the trim around the cross and it was amazing. There was a scripture on it that read: *He who finds a wife finds a good thing and obtains favor from the* Lord." (Proverbs 18:22). It looked good and I'm sure it would taste good. Both of our parents thought the cakes were beautiful and they made up in their minds they were going to pay for them for us as one of our wedding gifts. They would not take "no" for an answer.

I thought that I would take some time to myself to have a little lunch and think. I have been so busy working on the wedding that I have not had too much time to myself, outside of taking a shower and sleeping. This time in my life is so special, being the woman that I am and watching God bless me the way He has will always blow me away. I am more than grateful.

I drove over to the "Delicatessen" to have a sandwich and some chips. I wasn't in the mood for anything heavy. I got in line and waited to place my order, the line wasn't too long but of course I have to admit I wanted it to move along.

As I stood there being patient all of a sudden, someone walked up behind me kissed me on the cheek and said, "Hi there beautiful." I turned around and it was Kris!! I grabbed and hugged him as if I hadn't seen him in years. He looked absolutely wonderful. He had on some nice Levi jeans, a blue button down shirt that was crisp and starched just like he liked his shirts. He smelled good, his smile was as bright as always and he looked like he had just gotten his hair cut. Finally, I said "Hi honey, it is so good to see you. I can't believe we both came here to grab a bite." "I know", he said. "I was heading to the store to pick up a few things, and decided I'd stop here to get something quick." I responded by saying,

"I'm glad you did." We went ahead and sat at table since we may not have the time later.

"So, Mrs. Thompson are you nervous yet?" I looked at Kris and smiled and said "No, not yet and I don't have to be because God blessed me with the best man on this side of heaven." Kris smiled and held my hand; just as he touched my hand the waitress came over with our food. He looked up at her and said "Thank you". We talked a little and ate quickly as we had to keep on our schedules.

Kris walked me to my car and hugged me. "Well in a few hours we will be one, and I can't wait", Kris said. "Neither can I and Kris I pray that I am all you need me to be. I hope to see you later tonight." He kissed me on my cheek and helped me into my car. "I love you sweetheart", he said. We waved to one another and drove off. What a refreshing break in my day.

I have a few more things to get done, before meeting Samaria and getting to the church to go over a few things. I went to the mall to pick up my pantyhose, my jewelry and my shoes. This is not going to take too long because I know exactly where to go and what I want. I knew I wasn't going to go in browsing, because it would take more time than I can spare.

My pantyhose are ivory and glittery. My jewelry is a combination of pearls and rhinestones. The bracelet is rhinestones and pearls braided together and a ribbon ties it at the end. My earrings are circular with pearls and rhinestones between each pearl and one big rhinestone in the center. My necklace is braided like my bracelet with a silver bow hanging at the bottom with rhinestones in it and a ribbon ties it to. I think I will certainly give the appearance of royalty. Once I get my hair and make up done in the morning that will be it.

As I head home I call Samaria to make sure she is ready, I certainly don't want to be at the church all night. She answers the phone and l say, "Hey are you ready? I'm on my way". She chuckled and said, "Of course, I am always on time." "Alright, I'll be there in thirty minutes." I hung up and thought to myself, that Samaria was something else. She's a great cousin and more than that, a great friend.

I arrived home and ran in to change my shoes really quickly. Samaria was right there sitting in the living room waiting. I came right back out and we headed to the church, to make sure all was in place for the rehearsal dinner tomorrow night.

Kris had the wedding gifts for the bridal party and I had our parents' gifts. I think everyone will be very happy with their gifts. Kris and I picked them together and all of the gifts have a little of our personality in them.

I know that I have family that is coming from all over the United States and abroad. Our family stays in touch regularly, so it won't be like we haven't seen one another in years. At most it's been a year, even for the family that is abroad. My cousin Rajon is an international actor and he speaks six different languages. All of the films he's done are in foreign languages and he is awesome! Thank God for subtitles.

Malaysia lives in Dubai, India and is the V.P. of Marketing for a hotel chain. She runs a really tight ship, and she is well respected. When we were younger, she was always marketing something. There were five cousins that ran together, when we were teenagers and we will all be together again this weekend. Samaria (the God chaser, that inspires all of us); Malaysia (the God fearing business woman); Rajon (God's anointed actor); Malcolm (the God inspired author) and me (the new born soul). Yes, the "crumb snatchers" will be back together again and I am the last of the five to get married. I had no pressure though, because they all in some way have told me not to ever rush into marriage but to wait on God.

Samaria and I found that all was in order at the church, for the rehearsal dinner tomorrow night and we headed back home for some much needed rest and final prep time for me. Tomorrow night kicks off a new chapter in my life.

CHAPTER TWENTY

W hen Samaria, Mom and I drove up to the church who did we see, but the rest of the "crumb snatchers" standing out in the parking lot chatting it up. Once I parked the car it was on. Mom got out of the car and everyone hugged her first and we helped her into the church. After mom was inside, we screamed and hugged one another like little kids. It was so good to see them all again.

"OMG, my cousin is tying the knot tomorrow and I am so glad to be here to witness this great event", Malaysia said. Everybody laughed. "Hold on", Malcolm blurted out. "It's not because we didn't think it would happen, it's because we all agree it was a perfect time for all of us to be able to take off." "I can't wait to meet the lucky fella myself", Rajon said. "Let me hip you all early, he's a true gift from God. He's nothing but a gentleman and a lover of the Father." Samaria added.

We stood out in the parking for at least 30 minutes catching up and who pulled up but Kris. Samaria was like, "Alright troops, here comes the man of God now." "What? He's a Pastor?" Malaysia asked.

"No clown." Samaria said. "He's saved, so he's a man of God". Malcolm almost fell over laughing.

Kris pulled up right beside my car. I was so nervous. He got out of the car and walked up to me and gave me the best hug ever and said, "Hello Mrs. Thompson". I started cheesing from ear to ear and responded with a sweet, "Hello". He held me so tight. I could feel the love and the security in his arms. I looked him in his eyes and said, "I have some very special people I want you to meet. These are my cousins; we call each other the "crumb snatchers." He laughed.

I introduced him to everyone and he expressed how excited he was to have met them. We all talked outside for a few more minutes, before my Mom came out and said we had to get started. As we all walked in, we continued to laugh and talk. It was as if everyone had known Kris for years. We met Kris's family on the inside. They were already seated and talking amongst themselves. Kris introduced me to everyone I didn't know and I in turn introduced them to my family. Well, to tell the truth we are all family now.

The food smelled so good and everyone was so excited about the food they almost forgot about rehearsal. Pastor Gresham called us all together and we had prayer. Rehearsal began and when I say we

140

had so much fun, I mean it. Of course Samaria stood in for me, as I sat in my seat and thought about the fact that I would be in that spot tomorrow. Dad and Samaria had a great time walking down the isle, my Dad already thinks he's cool and Samaria thinks she's a DIVA so they had swag and stroll really going on.

There wasn't much to rehearsal and we were doing the traditional wedding vows so we didn't have to memorize anything. After Pastor Gresham said a few things, Kris and I shared our love and thanks for everyone coming and we gave our wedding party their gifts. They were all excited about what they received. All of the men received three pair of cufflinks, their tux, a money clip with their initials on it and a gift certificate for a round of golf at the Waddington Country Club. The women received hosiery for the wedding, their dress, earrings, necklace and bracelet, shoes and their hair would be done.

After giving the gifts, there were some greetings still being exchanged. Finally, Daphne called for everyone's attention and directed us all down to the fellowship hall for the dinner. Daphne had everyone wait until we got there, the doors were closed but I could tell that the lights were dim. When Daphne opened the door, I was amazed at how everything turned out. It was gorgeous. The ceiling looked like a starlit night. The tables were decorated with floral and candle center pieces. The flowers had fiber optic lights in the leaves and the place settings were cream colored plates with gold napkins and metallic gold napkin holders. The chairs were parsons' chairs with cream colored covers that tied in the back. It was absolutely beautiful. I could hear all of the comments and I think I saw tears welling up in Kris' eye. He was happy and I have to say I was elated. We walked to our table and the wedding party followed.

The staff that was serving us seated all of the remaining family and guest that were there. Dad said the prayer and the servers begin serving us. Before dinner everyone filled out the meal ticket choosing their soup and meat. With names and seat numbers on the meal ticket it was easier.

The musicians that were playing at the wedding were set up downstairs to play live music. That was a pleasant surprise. They played some soothing worship music and everyone enjoyed it.

The staff made sure Kris and I were served first, then our parents and the wedding party. The conversation around the table was incredible. There were great stories told about both Kris and I from our family and friends. We laughed and laughed hard. It was a wonderful evening.

I looked up for a minute and saw that the *"crumb snatchers"* were whispering in Daphne's ear. They were all smiling and looked to be up to something. Shortly after, Daphne went to the microphone. She announced we were having a special presentation.

All of them including Samaria come up to the front and Malaysia takes the microphone and speaks. "This weekend is a very special weekend for our family. Our cousin Passion is about to be married and we want Kris to know something." Rajon then comes up, "Kris before you even say I do, we want you to know that we believe in family and all it stands for. We are a praying, loving, caring, understanding and faith filled family. We're here for you just like we are here for Passion. We love you man and welcome to the family." Of course I was crying and everyone else was touched by his kind words.

I looked at the time and it was almost midnight. We were having such a great time talking and mingling, that time just flew by. I had to get home and get some rest because my hair appointment was early and I wanted to get to the church on time. Kris and I said our goodnights as Daphne, Samaria and a few others closed things down for us.

Kris and I said goodnight to one another in the parking lot and he followed me to a certain point and

I went the rest of the way home. Once I got home I got my things together for the wedding and I took a shower. I knew I would be asleep by the time everyone else got home. I looked around the house, knowing it would be my last night there. God blessed me with that house and it would be paid off in a few days and passed on to my sister so that she can have a place to raise her child.

I brushed my teeth, read a passage of scripture and started to drift off to sleep. As my eyes begin to close, my phone rang. "Hello", I said in a very tired voice. "Hi there Mrs. Thompson, I wanted you to know that I made it home and I love you. I look forward to our day tomorrow and I can't wait to whisk you away for a few days. Rest well my sweet bride." I smiled and said, "You to."

CHAPTER TWENTY ONE

My alarm clock went off at 6:00am and I had to get up to be at the salon by 7:30. I jumped into the shower again, because I knew it would be a hectic day. When I came out of the shower, I was surprised to see that Precious was lying in my bed waiting for me to come out. "Hey there sleepy head, what's up?" I said. She rubbed her eyes and said, "Nothing much, just wanted to spend a little time with you before you rushed off." I smiled and sat down beside her. "So, you are about to have your own home, paid in full. You won't have to buy any furniture unless you just want to. If you do, please promise me you'll find someone who needs furniture and give them what you are replacing." I said. Precious assured me she'd do that.

"Passion, are you happy?" Precious asked. I looked at her and was able to say without pausing, "Yes, I am very happy. Kris is a blessing from God. I am so glad he found me." "I am happy for you sis and I pray that you and Kris have a wonderful life together, just don't forget about me." Precious said. "Girl, we aren't moving out of state and we will still see one another through out the week. Of course, you know I'll be over often once the baby is born. You can't get rid of me kiddo." We hugged and I looked at the time and realized I had to go. I finished getting dressed, grabbed some toast and coffee, and looked in to see if Samaria was ready. She and I were going to the salon at the same time and the other ladies would be there a little later. The wedding starts at 12 noon and we have to be there at 10:30am for everyone to get their make up done. She was ready and we were on our way. Precious would come in a little bit with our cousins.

We arrived at the salon on time and we were the only ones there so Trina went right to work on my hair. She put in a relaxer and she worked it in. She shampooed Samaria's hair and as soon as she finished her, the ladies started showing up. I was glad they were on time. Trina shampooed me and put me under the dyer. I was the only one that was getting a relaxer everyone else was getting a shampoo and set. The salon was filled with excitement. I of course couldn't hear their conversation being under the dryer so I went into my own little world. I eventually drifted off to sleep.

Trina lifted the hood of the dryer and it seemed like a few minutes and I was out and ready to be styled. Samaria's dryer had stopped and she was next.

Things were running smoothly and we trying to make sure we were on time for everything. As Trina styled my hair I begin to see myself walking down the aisle. I was smiling inside and it felt good to know, that in a few hours I was going to marry a marvelous man. Trina said, "Alright Ms. Passion you are all done and ready to go." I responded with a hug and a thank you." Samaria was right behind me and we were on our way. We told the other ladies we'd see them at church.

It was 9:00am and we had an hour and a half so we grabbed a bite to eat via drive through. It was okay, because we knew we'd eat at the reception. The make-up artist was a prompt person so we didn't want to sit down to eat and risk running late.

We ordered and left. We got to the church at 10:05, the caterer was there setting up and the sexton was there doing some final cleaning. I looked in the sanctuary and the decorator was hard at work putting the flowers in their place, and the florist was placing a box of corsages and boutonnières on the lobby table for the bridal party. I could tell which ones belonged to Kris and I. My heart begins to beat really fast.

I went downstairs to First Lady Gresham's office, that's where I along with the ladies in the bridal party were getting dressed. Samaria had my gown and her dress and she hung them on the hook on the back of the office door. I had our shoes and the rest of our accessories and placed them on the sofa. We put on our under garments and our robes, took our shoes and jewelry out and waited for the other ladies to show up. When we left the salon, everyone was there. Precious was walking in, when we reached the car in the parking lot next to the salon.

Samaria looked at me and said, "Well cousin this is it. God's plan is finally coming together. I am happy for you and I want you to know that, this is just one day. The real test of your marriage begins after the wedding is over and after the family and friends are gone. You all have a strong support system in your families, but the real support comes from God. You have to keep Him, at the center of your marriage and not people. Also, be reminded that when God has ordained a thing, the enemy will take several shots at you so don't be surprised if old boyfriends and girlfriends show up out of nowhere, even here today.

You have to make sure you pray for your husband everyday and keep him covered. He will need it. I love you and I am so happy that I am your Matron of Honor." She reaches over and hugs me.

Right after Samaria finishes talking, in walks my Mom, Samaria's husband Mitchell and my make-up artist Daniel with his wife Portia. The reality of today has really set in now. Samaria rushed over to

Mitchell and gave him a hug and kiss. It is amazing what God has done for their marriage. If at any point in our marriage Kris and I experience some rough patches, I pray I can be as strong Samaria. She is an amazing woman and whether she knows it or not she is my mentor.

The wedding party has started to arrive. Not sure what's going on, on Kris' side but the ladies are in the room and Daniel and Portia are setting up to get started. He's fast but he wants to make sure he has plenty of time to get the brides maids first and save me for last.

My nerves are kicking in now and I pray I don't faint. My Mom notices and comes over to me. She takes my hand and says, "Baby, everything is going to be well. I can see that you are a little nervous, don't worry because this is the will of God." I smiled, my Mom always knows just what to say and when even if it makes you mad.

I took a deep breath and joined in the conversation with the ladies in the room. Samaria came back in, from having walked out into the hallway with Mitchell to chat and catch up on things. I asked, "So, how is your hubby?" She had this huge grin on her face and said, "Fine, can't you tell. He went to find the guys and he said he would text me and let me know how Kris is doing." At that point Daniel and

Portia called for another bridesmaid to come and sit in their chairs.

Things were moving pretty fast, I overheard someone say it was 11:15. Okay, so now my nerves are really on edge. In 45 minutes I will be walking down to the altar, starting a new phase in my life. I wonder how many guests are here. I pray everyone was able to come. Is Kris here? Everything I can imagine is running through my mind. Okay, time to take another deep breath and trust God to walk with me. I know for a fact that God does all things well. Why, shucks look at what He's done with me.

CHAPTER TWENTY TWO

The wedding party was ready. The ladies were gasping at me in my wedding gown and saying how beautiful I looked. The photographer snapped photos as each one of them gave me a kiss on the cheek and left the office to line up. I could hear the organ playing and people talking. Samaria stayed behind with me for a few more minutes, since she was the last one to walk down before the flower girls.

My nerves were really kicking in now. My Mom and Dad came in and at that time Samaria hugged me, said a quick prayer and went up stairs with the rest of the wedding party. My Mom looked at me with tears in her eyes, "Baby, this is a really big day and I trust that the Lord has directed you. I love you and I pray only God's best for you and Kris. Just because you will be married, doesn't mean you aren't still our baby". She hugged me and sat on the sofa. I knew what she meant, "We are still in charge and you can call on us anytime."

My Dad looked at me and smiled. "Baby girl, you look absolutely amazing. This is one of the hardest moments in a father's life, to hand his daughter over to another man to provide for her. For me today though, it feels right. I believe Kris is the man that God has sent to you and I know all will be well. We are about to take the longest stroll we have ever taken together, but one that will have a happy ending. Like your mother said, you are still our baby and we are here if you need us. Let's get ready for our stroll." I had to hold back my tears so I wouldn't mess up my make up. Dad and I hugged and I heard the music begin for the bridal party, it was 12:00 noon exactly. I took a deep breath and grabbed my Dad's arm.

As we walked upstairs, I was about to crumble. We stood at the bottom of the stairs until my Mom and Kris' Mom and Dad were walked in. My little cousin looked at me and smiled as she prepared to toss the rose petals. She had on a miniature dress like mine. Her brother looked handsome in his tuxedo as he carried the pillow with our actual rings on it. He assured me with thumbs up, that he wouldn't lose them.

The double doors leading into the sanctuary shut immediately behind him and at that point my Dad and Uncle help me up the stairs. My Aunt helped with my train and got me all together. I could hear the music, of all music begin to play. It was my time to walk down the aisle.

The double doors opened and the cameras started flashing. I put on my best smile and held tight to my

Dad's arm. I hear people's comments, some people were waving to make sure I knew they were there and I looked up and saw my husband to be smiling from ear to ear. He looked amazing, his tuxedo fit him perfectly. Not a hair was out of place. His shoes were not the regular tuxedo shoes, he wore his own black polished tie up loafer style shoe. He was cleanly shaven and his dimples were calling my name.

I took my eyes off of Kris for only a second and looked directly into the eyes of Terry. What was he doing here? I didn't tell him about the wedding. He smiled and that smile of his was a killer. He even slightly winked at me. I turned away quickly and looked directly at Samaria, she nodded as if to say, "I see him girl, don't worry I'm praying." Seeing Terry, really threw me off kilter.

I managed to get myself back focused. As I passed by Terry he said, "Wow, you look great!" I almost stumbled, but my Dad had me. I could smell Terry's cologne and I so wanted to look him in his face. Why? I have no idea.

I made it to the altar and now I am all frazzled. Pastor Gresham began the ceremony. "Dearly beloved, we are gathered here today in the sight of God and all of these witnesses." It was as if time stood still. My mind was wondering, why would

Terry show up here? Oh, I hate that he came. I wonder who he came with, probably that under dressed girl next to him. Wait, why am I so concerned about who he came with, I'm about to have a husband. At that moment I heard the words, "Who gives this women to be married to this man?" My Dad steps forward and says, "Her Mother and I". He turned and hugged me, and then he hugged Kris and placed my hand in Kris' hand and walked to his seat. That was it, no longer Daddy's girl but Kris' wife.

We stood before Pastor Gresham as he spoke and then came the dreaded statement, *"If anyone knows why these two should not be wed, speak now or forever hold your peace"*. I heard Terry clear his throat. I dare not look back. No one said anything and Pastor Gresham said, "Praise God, you all passed your first test." The guest all laughed.

Pastor Gresham looked down at Rodney and said, "May I have the rings son?" He carefully handed the pillow to his Dad (Malcolm) and when he had it in his hands, everyone clapped. Pastor took the rings and blessed them as we placed them on one another's' finger. The rings were beautiful and if I must say so myself, my ring looked nice on my hand, all three carats.

After we placed our rings on, we kneeled for Communion and prayer. We walked over once done and lit the Unity Candle. We both gave our mother's a rose. I hugged them both and begin to cry. Samaria was right there with a handkerchief to dry my face. As we stood back in front of Pastor Gresham, there was hush over the guest. Pastor Gresham spoke, "Well, we have come to everyone's favorite part of the ceremony including the Bride and Groom." There was laughter.

"Alright, Kris", Pastor Gresham says. You may salute your bride. Kris takes my veil and pulls it back from my face. He looks me in my eyes and says, "Passion, I love you and I thank God for giving you to me. Today begins a beautiful journey and I plan to do all I can with the strength of God to make it a joyful one." I of course begin to cry and he places his hands on my cheeks and kisses me. The crowd went wild, especially the "Crumb Crushers". I can now turn to the guest and say, "I's married now". I didn't. I felt so much joy and as we were introduced to everyone it was a great feeling. "Ladies and gentlemen, I introduce to you for the first time "Mr. and Mrs. Kris Thompson". The crowd goes wild again, what an awesome feeling to have so much love and support.

We walk down the aisle waving and smiling. I look to my left and Terry has this awful look on his face. The girl now, standing behind him places her hand on his shoulder and he pushes it off. Wow, what a position to be in. I kept it moving.

Kris and I went off to Pastor's office which was upstairs, until they cleared the sanctuary for us to come back in and take photos. We enjoyed our alone time as we embraced one another and share a few kisses. It was amazing and I mean amazing. For me it was incredible, standing there with a man I had never "KNOWN". I laugh to myself and in my mind I say, "I'll know him later."

Pastor Gresham knocks on the office door and tells us the cost is clear to come out and take our pictures. We emerge and the wedding party begins to applaud. We take in every moment and Kris starts to show his silly side, by pulling his collar and saying, "I know I hit the jack pot." Smiling and cheesing like J. J. Evans. The picture taking began and we had a ball.

CHAPTER TWENTY THREE

Everyone lined up upstairs in the order we were being introduced. We put the kids in the front of the line, so they could be seated first. Our friends James and Regina Howard ("The Sweethearts of the Industry"™) were the hosts for our reception. They had a very unique way of introducing each couple. They found out something about each wedding party member and used it to introduce them. The couples had no idea, but they loved it.

When they introduced us, they came from behind their podium and stood beside us and said, *"Ladies and Gentlemen please welcome the new "Sweethearts" on the scene Mr. and Mrs. Kris Thompson."* They gave us a huge hug and we invited them to sit at the head table with us. They are an awesome transparent couple that desires only the best for other couples. Now, that Kris and I are married we are going to attend their annual marriage conference, *"In Love in Him....After we Say I Do"*.

After our introduction, we were instructed to stand in front of the wedding party table and at that time we received our guests. The wedding party came down and joined us. Samaria stood next to me and we looked at each other and smiled. I was happy and she was happy for me.

The receiving line started, everyone was so nice and I couldn't believe all of the financial gifts we were receiving. As I finished greeting some family members, I looked up and who was standing in front of me but Terry. I all but passed out.

I couldn't act any different, so I shook his hand and hugged him. He whispered in my ear, "You know you should be wearing that wedding dress with me. You look stunning in it to." I backed away slightly so that I could look in his face and said, "You were not invited Terry why are you here?" He laughed, "Because we haven't had closer and I thought we were still an item. You never ended things with me." Kris was talking to someone else and had not noticed us talking yet. "Terry, we were not in a relationship and this is not the time for you to barge in and want to talk. If you have something to say, we can do it in about two weeks. Now, please leave me alone. "He looked at me and smiled, "We will have that talk", he whispered and walked away.

I was so thrown off at that point. Kris touched me on my hand and asked, "Sweetheart are you alright?" I nodded and said, "Yes" at the same time. We had just a few more guests to greet and the newlyweds could sit down and eat. I needed something after that stint with Terry.

The receiving line was done and we all took our seats at the head table. It was such a joy to get off of my feet.

Everything was absolutely beautiful and I couldn't wait to dig in. As we all ate, of course there was some good conversation going on. Every now and again someone would tap the side of their drinking glass so that Kris and I could share a kiss. We didn't mind at all.

The wedding party was having a great time laughing and talking. Kris and I made our rounds to our guests. As we walked and talked we got so much advice and of course the most popular was: "Don't go to bed angry". We had already planned on making sure we prayed together before going to bed and settling any issues we may have had during the day.

The reception was great, but I have to say that I was so tired. I wanted to get on the plane and head to Aruba. I could picture us in the hotel and on the beach. I really wanted to take my shoes off and put my feet up. I believe Kris was feeling the same way.

There was a tapping of the glass and Kris and I shared a kiss. The crowd seems to love that. Our Best man stood up to make a comment, "I am so honored to have shared in this wonderful day, with Kris and Passion and I pray God's blessings on their future. At this time I would like to invite them to the dance floor for the first dance." Everyone begin to applaud, as we walked down to the dance floor. The DJ played our favorite song, by Stevie Wonder "Knocks Me off My Feet". We shared a beautiful dance and I so wanted to bail the reception afterwards. We only had a few more minutes and then we could go to the hotel and leave for our honeymoon mid morning. "Yes, I'm ready".

The servers were taking up the plates and the guests were heading to the dance floor, for the last dance. Yup, you guessed it "Cupid's Shuffle". Kris and I laughed so hard, because we just knew we would get out of the reception without doing a line dance. We realized that church folks like to have a good time to. We all gathered on the floor and did the best "Cupid Shuffle" ever. It seems like, when people dance together or have church together they forget about all of their differences and enjoy themselves.

Daphne came and tapped Kris and I on the shoulder and told us we had to throw the bouquet and the garter and head to the hotel. That sounded good to us. We eased out of the dance line, and James and

Regina got all of the single ladies attention for the throwing of the bouquet. They only needed to say it once; they all came running to the center of the floor. I stood there with the bouquet in my hand and wanting so badly to turn around and see who I could throw it to. I know that would have been cheating. All of the ladies were ready so I did what all brides do, I faked the first throw. You would think they would know that one by now. Finally, I threw the bouquet and guess who caught it, yup, "Precious". It was easy; because she was pregnant no one would push her out of the way. She knew she was going to catch it. We took our photo together with huge smiles on our faces.

It was now the men's turn. They all came to the center of the floor. Many of them had taken their coats off, because they were ready to use a few football moves. When I turned around to look, Terry was front and center. Samaria caught my eye and some how gave me a little comfort. I could not believe how bold he was and I most definitely could not believe he caught it. Now he was taking a picture with Kris. You know his smile was huge.
Me not having to take a picture with him, made it alright.

Samaria, grabbed Kris by the arm and walked him over to me. We held hands as we said our good nights. Daphne and Paul got the gifts and cards from the gift table and loaded the cars to bring them to the house. Kris and I actually went to a downtown hotel for the night. Our bags were already there packed and ready to go to the airport in the morning. The "crumb snatchers" were going to help unpack at the house and other things were going to be delivered while we were gone. Samaria and Mitchell stayed at our house until we returned. Paul was going to go by and help with the unpacking. He would be gone once I got back from the honeymoon.

As we exited the reception, our guests were there with their bird seeds throwing them as we got into the limo. We kissed our parents and gave a few hugs and headed to the hotel. No one knew where we were staying except Samaria, Mitchell and Daphne and we knew our secret was safe with them.

The driver took off and we looked and waved out of the back window until we couldn't see them any more. Kris turned to me and said, "I love you Mrs. Thompson". "I love you Mr. Thompson", I replied. Our new life together has begun.

CHAPTER TWENTY FOUR

We were awakened by our hotel wake up call. It felt like we had just drifted off to sleep. We had to get right up, because our flight leaves at 11:00am and the airport was at least thirty minutes away. Kris slowly opened his eyes and looked right into mine. "Good morning, sweetheart", he said. "Good morning", was my reply. I got up and brushed my teeth, showered and got dressed. Kris was right behind me. He got up and got ready. We didn't have to really pack anything, Samaria and Mitchell were going to come by hotel and check us out. They were picking up our over night things, Kris' tuxedo and my wedding gown and taking them to the house and dropping the hotel room key off at the front desk. We put those things together, the do not disturb sign on the door and they had the second key. We left our key on the dresser by the television.

We took the hotel shuttle to the airport and we were on our way to the honeymoon of a life time. Kris had his arm around me the entire ride. As we were riding to the airport, Kris pulled a gift box out of his jacket pocket and handed it to me. I asked, "Honey, what is this?" He told me to just open the box. I did and it was the most beautiful gold and diamond cross necklace I had ever seen. I hugged him and tried to control my emotions on the shuttle. I was so surprised.

We arrived at the airport at 9:45am and had enough time to check our bags and make it to our gate. We stopped at Dunkin Doughnuts for some coffee and a bagel with strawberry cream cheese. We sat down at our gate with no carry on bags at all, just the breakfast snack we were sharing. We knew we would have breakfast on our flight, since we were flying first class. We were about to board, so we prayed before they called for our flight.

It was 10:30am when we begin to board. The gate agent was making her announcements and my phone buzzed; I took it out, only to see a text message from Terry. I didn't read it, I just closed the alert. When Kris asked me "If someone was calling?", I told him "No, I was checking to make sure my phone was on vibrate before we boarded the plane". Already, I am lying to my husband. "Help me Lord".

The gate agent called for all first class passengers and Kris and I got up with tickets and passports in hand. The agent checked our tickets and IDs and let us board. Finally, we were on our way. They announced that we would be leaving a little early and that was alright with us.

It didn't take them long to finish boarding and seating the other passengers, before they told us we would be taxing down the run way shortly. We sat in the front seats (A and B) and it was almost immediate when the flight attendant asked if she could get us something to drink. We both asked for water and coke. I was able to eat a little now since the wedding was over. I had been dieting and taking
it easy on the grub.

The Captain came on the loud speaker, gave us our flight schedule and told us that we were third in line for take off. The flight attendant was taking our breakfast order and I was getting comfortable for the long flight. Anything over an hour and a half was long to me. She got our order and we had our food within ten minutes. Kris and I finished up and it was time for our much needed nap. We were hoping to sleep all the way there, that would be great if we did.

We called Samaria and Mitchell right before we boarded to let them know we were on our way. Samaria said she and Mitchell would be going by the hotel around 11:30am. They wanted to get over there and back to the house so they could start setting things set up for us. We told them not to do everything, leave something for us to do when we get back. She agreed.

The Pilot speaking woke Kris and I from our sleep and we were glad to know we had landed in Aruba. Yes, time to relax, swim, eat and play. We both joined hands before exiting the plane and thanked God for a safe flight. We were the first ones off of the plane and we nearly ran to baggage claim. We were both excited about this honeymoon/vacation.

Kris got our bags and to my surprise had a limo waiting for us. The driver had a sign with our name on it. We had a nice long drive to the resort and when we got there it was absolutely beautiful.

We checked in and prepared for a night of dinner and dancing. Kris had already checked out the restaurants, so our first night out was going to be a surprise.

Kris changed into a white linen outfit and I changed into a white linen dress. We were casual, just cute and comfortable. Kris had on some tan sandals and I had on some tan and white sandals with a cute little tan and white purse to match. My hair was set for the week in Aruba. Trina wrapped and pinned me up really good. I had my satin scarf to tie it up and it was not moving.

At dinner we ordered some shrimp and Kris knew that I loved crab legs and ordered three pounds between the two of us. We also had fried clams and oysters. We had virgin tropical drinks and did a little dancing at the restaurant. Before heading back to our room, we took a nice little stroll on the beach. I have to admit we had a great night and I was ready for a good night sleep (wink).

Kris wanted to play a few rounds of golf today and he set that up. It would be my first time playing, but I was willing to learn. I also looked cute in my little golf outfit. We were going to play tennis sometime before we left Aruba and that outfit is super hot.

One thing I have always loved about my hubby is that my weight never bothered him. I am a plus size women but I handle and carry myself well. I made and will continue to make sure I keep myself up. Being plus size doesn't mean I have to let myself go.

After our fun round of golf, we came back to the hotel to shower rest, shop and do dinner. Kris went in to take his shower first. I was sitting on the bed when my phone vibrated. I thought it may be my Mom or Dad, so I just answered. It was Terry. "Hi there beautiful, you miss me?" Quickly, I responded, "Terry I am a married woman, why are you calling me?" I checked to see if Kris had gotten out of the shower. He hadn't. "You sound a little nervous. Does your husband know that you are on the phone with me?" I paused before answering him. "What is wrong with you Terry? I asked. "Are you trying to

167

ruin my marriage?" He laughed and said, "Ruin you isn't what I want to do. I only want the best for you. You left me hanging though. We were still an item; you said one thing but did another. What kind of Godly woman are you?" I was appalled at his comment. "How dare you try to make me look bad? I told you it was over between us but you didn't seem to understand. You know what?, I don't have time to fool around with you, I'm on my honeymoon with the man I love and the man God sent to me. Stop calling me Terry and I mean it!" I slammed the phone down and just in the nick of time. Kris came out of the shower and walked up behind me and gave me a really big hug. He kissed me on the neck and said, "Your turn honey, we've got to get a move on." I smiled and at the same time prayed he didn't hear me on the phone. I quickly said, "I'm off and I'll be right back." I felt like such a phony. I shouldn't feel bad though, I am not in a relationship with Terry and he has no right to try and tell me how to handle my life. Who does he think he is? I told myself to breath as I got into the shower. I had to let go of this nonsense.

I stepped out of the shower to find my handsome husband laying across the bed waiting for me. I dried off and begin to dress, when Kris asked, "Are you alright honey. You seem a little distant?" I was surprised at him asking me anything, because I thought I was covering my feelings pretty good.

After a brief stint of silence, I said "I'm fine honey; I think the flight really got the best of me. My energy should boost up again after I get you back out on the dance floor." He chuckled and jumped up off of the bed and put his arms around me and gave me a kiss. He pulled back and looked into my eyes and said, "I am so grateful to God for allowing you to bump into me in the hallway, you are the greatest thing to happen to me in a very long time. I promise God I will do all I can to make sure I add to your happiness. You are my true rib girl." Talk about a lump in the throat, I had one. How could he feel that way about me and my little secret? Oh, I know I will have to tell him about Terry sooner or later. Right now I am thinking it will have to be later.

I put on a cute little colorful sundress and grabbed my shoes as we headed out to bring a wonderful end to our day. Kris took me by my hand and we strolled in the breeze to the restaurant of my choice tonight. We were off to another fantastic night of dining and who knows what else, all I know is I am having a great time and I wasn't going to let anyone or anything ruin it for me.

CHAPTER TWENTY FIVE

I cannot believe our time in Aruba was up. We had such a wonderful time enjoying each other and the many things we did while here. We had an early flight back home and we were excited about our new beginning in our new house. I know Precious was doing well, having adjusted to a fully furnished paid off house. Our parents believe in leaving things within the family and leaving a legacy for our children.

Kris and I have already started a fund for our yet to be born child(ren). Every pay check we will both deposit $50.00 into an account and once we have a child, change the account over into their name. We want to be prepared. We can draw from that account to help with child care and other things that relate to our child, we will also continue to make deposits.

Before leaving for the airport we called Samaria and Mitchell to let them know we were on our way. Mitchell answered and we could tell they were asleep, "Good morning", he said. "I replied all chipper, "Good morning, we were just calling to let you guys know we are heading to the airport." "Cool", he said. "What time does your flight land?" I looked at my ticket and answered, "10:18 am". Mitchell said they would be there on time to pick us up.

We gave the room one last once over, took a few more pictures, both in the room and in the lobby and then checked out. We boarded the shuttle to the airport and we were on our way.

The airport was crowded, thank goodness we were not flying stand by because we would not get on. We wanted to get back and make sure all was in order before we returned to work. We had four more days off and we were going to enjoy getting settled in.

We checked our bags and headed for our gate. We are avid coffee drinkers, so we got a cup before boarding and enjoyed it while we waited. Kris pulled out the camera and we took a few pictures in the airport. The people there were so friendly; it's hard to believe that a young woman went missing here a few years ago.

The gate agent called for our plane to board and of course being in first class we were seated early. Boarding was easy because I only had a purse, so no opening any overheads for us.

The service going back home was just as good as it was coming over. We finally sat back and we both went to sleep, when I woke up we were landing. I tapped Kris on his shoulder and he woke up. We got ourselves together and prepared to get off of the plane.

Even though we had not made it to our house yet, being back in the city was a great feeling. It's good to go away, but coming home is always great. "Home, sweet home".

Mitchell and Samaria were at baggage claim waiting for us with smiles on their faces. We hugged one another and grabbed the bags. Mitchell and Kris rode in the front and Samaria and I sat in the backseat and caught up. She of course wanted to know all that went on while we were gone. I couldn't share everything so I shared just enough. I told her, that the four of us would have to go there for a vacation get away sometime in the not so distant future. She agreed and suggested we open it up to our cousins. I thought that would be great.

After a nice little ride, finally we were home. We hadn't been in the house since the walk through and the closing. Kris rented out his house and I let Precious stay in mine, until she was ready to move out into something of her own.

The lawn looked fantastic; Mitchell does a wonderful job with landscaping. I have told him so many times, he should start his own business. He doesn't have to work, just hire some good workers, get a couple of trucks and let the Lord handle it from there. He is great handling business so he would be able to land some great business and residential contracts.

When Kris and I walked into the foyer, we were elated because from where we were standing we could see that all of the curtains had been put up. The marble floor at the entrance of the house was beautiful, we ordered it a week before the wedding and they put it down the Monday after. They also laid the hardwood flooring; it was all just like we wanted it. The furniture arrived the Sunday after the wedding. We ordered bedroom furniture for four bedrooms, living room furniture, den furniture, Dining room furniture, a dinette set for the kitchen, various pieces for the finished basement, pieces for the foyer and other open areas, two queen sized beds and two six drawer chests for the bedrooms in the basement. The pool table was going to be delivered tomorrow.

The men that delivered the furniture set it all up and even helped Mitchell set up the mirrored weight room. I'm sure Mitchell and Samaria tried the weights out.

We loved everything about the house. The builder let us know if we had any issues to please give him a call once we got back in town. Aside from the normal warranty he was willing to do some extra things for us. He was a friend of Mr. Pittman's, so he was adding a lot of extras for us as a wedding gift. God is an awesome God!

All we had to do was unpack and go through the gifts and address thank you notes. Samaria and I planned on cooking dinner and letting the men relax. I was excited about using our new dishes, but paper plates sounded much better and I was totally down for that. Besides, Samaria had purchased some really fancy plastic plates.

I went up to the bedroom to change clothes and Kris was laid out across the bed fast asleep. I kissed him on the forehead, changed my clothes and laid down right beside him. We woke up two hours later from a knock on the bedroom door saying, "Dinner is ready." We looked at one another and just laughed. "Coming", Kris said. We washed our face and hands and headed down for a meal that smelled really good.

Once we got downstairs, Mitchell just shook his head and said, "Somebody has jet lag." "More than lag", Kris responded. "I feel like I haven't slept in days." I chimed in with, "A good nap does the body good".

Samaria and Mitchell cooked a good dinner; they served us up some smothered chicken, collard greens, homemade mashed potatoes, cornbread, sweet tea and homemade Red Velvet cake for dessert. Talk about having the "itis". I will have it right after I am done eating. The place was silent the entire meal, at one point we all just looked up. We all knew what that meant. We had to bow down to Samaria, for a very good meal.

All of the women in our family can cook, we all started cooking when we were about eight years old. Our Mom's had us on step stools helping put in the ingredients. I made my first pan of corn bread when I was ten. I mixed it up, but my Mom had to put it in the oven. Dad didn't want me near the stove to soon. Once Mom served it at dinner, Dad smiled and said, "The apple doesn't fall far from the tree." I knew that meant I did a good job and I wanted to cook all the time after that. When all of us cousins got together we would talk about what we had cooked that week. All of us did well and we were not in competition.

I helped Samaria clean up and put away the leftovers. Once we were done, we joined the men out on the deck. It was a beautiful day. There was a nice breeze and the sun was setting. As we got comfortable, Kris' cell phone rang. That was so funny, because it didn't ring at all while we were on our honeymoon. He walked back in the house to take it. He came back out a few minutes later and He didn't seem very happy.

"Honey, what's wrong?" I asked. He looked at me and said, "That was my job, they were calling to tell me I need to go out of town on Wednesday. They apologized because they realize I just came back from my honeymoon, but something came up and being the Supervisor I have to go." He looked so sad. Samaria said, "Kris, we will stay here with your bride while you are gone. I know that does not change how you may feel, but a man has to do what a man has to do."

Of course Kris has a smile on his face. He takes me by my hands and says, "Honey, I am so sorry about this but I promise I will make it up to you. I at least wish you could go with me." "It's okay and I know you will. This isn't going to happen often is it?" I asked. Kris quickly replied, "No, it won't and I'll see to that." "Where are you going anyway?" "To New Mexico", he said.

The remainder of the night was kind of quiet, but we still had a good time. At least Kris and I had two more days together before he left. I made up my mind that I was going to make the best of this time and enjoy my husband before he left. Besides, things do come up and we have to be willing to work it out.

CHAPTER TWENTY SIX

Today was a very busy day. We did some work around the house, ran some errands, made some phone calls and we went to see our parents. They knew we were back, but they wanted to give us some time to ourselves. Since Kris was leaving in the morning, we figured we should pay them a visit.

They were so excited about seeing us, it felt like it had been at least month, considering that we speak to our parents every day.

We talked about the honeymoon and then we dropped the bomb on them that Kris was going out of town on business. Everyone's reaction was just like ours, they understood but was concerned about me. I told them, "I'm fine, I don't want him to go but I know it's for work and he'll be back before we know it." As long I was okay, so was everyone else. Thank goodness Kris wasn't a Pastor/Evangelist; I could not deal with that kind of travel. I don't know how First Ladies handle their husbands being gone all of the time. God knew who to let marry a preacher and I wasn't one of those women.

Once we visited both of our parents we stopped to talk a little. We talked about him going away and Kris really wanted to know how I felt. I told him that I was honestly okay and I wanted him to be as well.

I pray that our communication will be like this throughout our marriage, it makes for a great relationship. There was a park across the street from the ice cream shop, so we went and sat on the park bench and watched the people that were passing by. If you want a really good laugh, just take a seat some where and watch the people. They are really, interesting.

We finished our ice cream and our conversation and headed back home. Before we got to the car, my cell phone rang. It was my parents. I answered with, "Hi, Mom/Dad what's up?" "Hi sweetheart", Mom said. "It's Precious, she's on her way to the hospital, can you all meet us? This may be it." I told my Mom, that Kris and I were on the way. When I hung up from Mom, I called Samaria and Mitchell, they told us to come back home and they would drive their car. We agreed taking two cars wouldn't make much sense. We dropped our car off and went straight to the hospital.

My parents were in the waiting room when we arrived. "Is she alright?" I asked. "Yes, baby girl she is doing great. She was asking for you a few minutes ago." "She was asking for me? I have no idea why, because I don't know nothing about birthing no babies." Everyone laughed including the staff that was in the waiting room.

At that moment, the doctor came out and asked "If Passion was here yet?" I answered, "Yes, I am". She said, "Great, I think you should come on in because she is not going to deliver this baby without you." I left my things with Kris and went back with the doctor. When I walked into the room the nurse gave me a robe and I had to sanitize my hands. Precious saw me and lit right up. "Hey sis, I am so glad you are back. I hope you don't mind that I wanted you in here with me." I kind of paused and then said, "Girl, you know I am not good at this kind of thing. You would have been better off having Mom come in here. I am lost." Precious laughed, but that may have caused a labor pain. She made this awful face and grabbed her stomach. After seeing her, I don't think this is something I want to go through. Kris and I will have to pray. I want kids but this is making me think twice.

The nurse came in and checked Precious again, she looked at her and said, "It's time young lady. You are about to be a Mommy. Let me go out to the desk and get your doctor. Are you going to in for the birth miss?" "Uh, yes I think so", I replied. I texted Kris and told him it was about to happen, I could hear

179

cheers coming from the waiting room. I knew he had told them what was in my text.

Precious asked me to get Mom and hold her. The doctor told her what she wanted her to do. The baby was about three weeks early, so Precious was thinking the baby was going to be sick. She was nervous, but Mom was praying.

Finally, after about forty-five minutes the baby's head crowned and the doctor comforted Precious by saying, "Okay, Precious just about two more pushes should do it." She held my hand tighter and we counted while she pushed, one, two, three, four, five. She took another deep breath and pushed again, out the baby came, a bouncing baby girl. She didn't look so good at the beginning, but after they cleaned her up she was beautiful. She weighed in at 7lbs 8ounces.

The nurse placed her in the arms of a very excited Precious. She was not crying because of labor pains now, but because she was happy she had a healthy baby girl. I don't think I have ever seen her smile so hard. Precious asked me to go get the rest of the family, after the doctor said it was okay to bring them in.

I took off my gown and walked out to the waiting room. Everyone except Kris had dozed off. Once I started talking they woke up. I told them that

Precious wanted to see them and we all went into the room.

Precious was groggy, but managed to say hi and hug everybody. "Mommy", she said "This was the experience of a life time. I know I am not married and I apologize to everyone for any shame I may have caused". She was assured all was well. "The birth of my daughter has truly changed me. I wanted you all to be here when I named her. I have found that a name says a lot about a person; therefore I have chosen to name my daughter, Michaela Brianne Taylor". We all sighed and ultimately, shared how much we loved the name she had chosen. We all stayed there for at least another hour, but we left because we knew Precious needed some rest and the baby needed to be poked, prodded, finger and foot printed. We shared our hugs, kisses and good byes with Precious and went home.

As we rode home, we all talked about how cute the baby was and how tired Precious looked. Not only was that in our forefront, but I think we were all in that, wow we may have a baby sometime in our very near future mode. Happy thought, but scary at the same time.

The four of us sat up and talked for a while, once we got back to the house. It was so good to see everyone at the hospital, it was hectic but we were able to catch up and Kris and I let them know that we had a great honeymoon.

Knowing that my honey was leaving the next morning, we wanted to get a little more alone time and we were about to make it happen. We didn't have to leave and go anywhere because we had a nice sitting room in our master bedroom, which was quite cozy. I made us some flavored coffee, cut us a slice of wedding cake and bought it upstairs so we could cuddle up and munch.

As we sat there, I looked at Kris and thought how amazing he was and I was going to miss him. I wasn't going to make a big deal, about him having to leave he has to work.

Kris popped in the movie "Just Wright". I got closer, laid my head on his shoulder and enjoyed our quality time. The things some women do, to get a man when they don't mean him any good. At some point we have to let go of the college conversations, grow up and realize a happy, healthy relationship isn't about money and fancy cars. I praise God for finally growing up.

CHAPTER TWENTY SEVEN

Kris was up early for his flight, he decided to drive himself to the airport just in case he came back early. I was cool with that, but you better know I was on his heels like a little puppy.

While he was putting his bag together, I went downstairs to make him some coffee and a bagel. He loves Dunkin Doughnuts' coffee, so I made sure Samaria got a bag from Walmart along with some travel coffee cups so he wouldn't have to stop off and buy any on his way to work. I put some strawberry cream cheese on his bagel and wrapped it up for him.

When I went back upstairs he was in the shower and I could hear him praying: *"Father in Jesus name, while I am away on this business trip cover my wife, and our home with your blood. Cause this meeting to be successful and bring business to the company that we didn't expect. As I travel through the air, guide the plane and keep the pilot focused. Give us safe passage there and back. Thank you for a new day and put me in the right place at the right time to share your love with someone I'll meet on the way. In Jesus name I pray, Amen."*

I was so grateful to God for a praying husband. I have to make it clear that he didn't just pray because he was leaving, but he prayed every morning. I make sure I pray every morning as well. One of the wives at the church told me about a conference call prayer group called *"Wailing Wives"*. They pray every Wednesday morning from 6:00am – 6:30am for their husbands and marriages. She said so many marriages have been blessed by this ministry. The one thing I found interesting, is that not every wife on the call may be having issues with her husband; they call just to keep their husbands covered in prayer.

Kris was all packed and ready to go; I was starting to feel a little sad. We've only been married a few days and already we were going to be separated. I grabbed his coffee and bagel and he grabbed his two bags.

He sat the bags at the door and gave me the best hug and kiss ever. He said, "I'll call you baby once I land and of course every night before I go to bed. I'm going to miss you. I love you gotta go now." I held the tears back and responded, "I love you and will miss you to baby." We kissed and my sweetheart left.

I stood and watched through the window until he was out of my sight. I went into the kitchen, poured myself a cup of coffee and made a bagel. I sat there and promised myself I was not going to cry nor was I going to call Kris. At that moment the home phone rang. I answered, "Hello". "Hey baby, it's me I just wanted you to know I miss you already." "Awww, Kris I miss you to." My baby called me, I feel fine now. I hug up the phone and begin to dance around the kitchen singing, "My baby loves me, yes he does." I was singing so loud that I woke Samaria up; she came into the kitchen and turned on the main light I only had the stove light on.

"Good morning cousin, what's going on you alright?" She said. "Oh, girl I am so sorry I woke you. Kris just called me to tell me he missed me and I was just so excited. He hadn't been gone an hour before he called me. Truth be told I really wanted to call him, but didn't want him to think I was a baby." Samaria laughed, "Oh my goodness, you all have the bug. I mean really, you all have been together for almost a year and somebody would think you all had just met and about three months ago. It's cool though, it should be that way and we pray that you will always find a way to keep fire and passion in your marriage." Passion is my name and for sure I wanted passion in my marriage.

It amazes me that when I was single, my girlfriends and I would get together for girls night out and chat it up about what we are going to do when we get married. However, after so many of those girlfriends got married all of that fire vanished. They felt burned out. Working, cooking, taking care of the kids and now divorced. I do not plan on being in that number. It is my plan to do all I can to make sure my husband is a satisfied man. He was happy when we met, and I want to add to his happiness.

I had to wait at the house for a bit, because we had more furniture being delivered today. While I was waiting I planned on finishing up a few things around the house. I wanted to use the new waffle iron we got as a gift, but I will have to wait a few more days to do that. I will however, put the wall fixtures up in the upstairs hallway and on the walls downstairs in the basement.

Samaria and Mitchell are planning to go out and do some shopping because they are staying over two extra weeks. Having them here is a blessing and it keeps me from being alone now that Kris is gone.

I headed upstairs to one of the bedrooms to go through the gifts and get the fixtures to put up when the doorbell rang. Mitchell was up so he answered it and wouldn't you know they were bringing the bedroom furniture for the four bedrooms, living room, den, Dining room, a dinette set for the kitchen, various pieces for the finished basement, pieces for the foyer and other open areas, two full size beds and two six drawer chests for the bedrooms in the basement. I was surprised, they were here so early. The pool table is scheduled to be delivered later today.

This was going to take a while and Mitchell said he would handle it and make sure they put everything in the proper place. I remained upstairs putting up the wall fixtures. Samaria came in to help me empty a few more boxes that had bathroom items, candles, vases and beautiful plush bath towels. One of our bathrooms was olive green and gold. The towels were a lighter green and would go great in that bathroom. Samaria put them in there for me. Kris was going to be excited to see the house coming together, when he gets home.

When I finally took a break, two and a half hours had passed. The gentlemen from the furniture company were bringing the last six drawer chest in. I made them all coffee to go and signed off on the paper work. They thanked us and we thanked them.

Samaria and Mitchell had to go run their errands so they showered and got dressed. They told me they would be gone for about three or four hours. That was fine I would make good use of my time. I was going to wait for the pool table to come, so I was not going out at least not anytime soon.

I went down to the kitchen to get a glass of water and figured I'd put away some of our kitchen gifts. The china we were given was absolutely beautiful and I wanted that to go in our china cabinet. It wouldn't only be for display, we will definitely eat off of it.

Time sure does fly when you're unpacking your new house. I got the kitchen all together and headed down to the basement when the doorbell rang. When I looked through the peep hole it was the recreation store delivering the pool table and they were early. I let them in through the back basement door, because it would be much easier to get the table in that way. They only had to put the legs on. It was a nice table and Kris was going to have a great time playing on it. After they put the legs on, they checked it out real good and hit a couple of balls. Yes, this is awesome and my baby will be glad. He's going to teach me how to play and we are going to be a fierce team.

I am done for the day. I am going to take a nice long hot bath and just relax. I got the phone, grabbed my bath pillow, some bath oil and bath gel and lit some candles. Lying back in the tub, I knew this was going to be just what I needed and I took advantage of this time.

CHAPTER TWENTY EIGHT

As soon as I closed my eyes, wouldn't you know it the phone rang. It was my baby. "Hi, honey I am so sorry I didn't call you. When I got to the airport, they were boarding the flight early and I had to get right on. I am on my way to the hotel and I will be going into my session about an hour after I arrive. Please don't be upset with me."

"I'm not upset with you honey, I am glad you a safe arrival and I miss you." "I know these few days are going to be busy, but I can't wait to get back home to you." I was glad to hear from him, I know I was going to rest well now.

"I promise I will call you tonight before I go to bed." I will be waiting up for your call. I love you sweetheart. Enjoy your meeting." "I love you to baby, bye-bye," he said.

I tell you that man is so wonderful. I don't know how I landed him. Thank you Lord for my awesome gift. Kris is the best thing that has ever happened to me.

After we finished our short conversation Samaria and Mitchell came in. They looked like they were extremely tired. "Hey guys," I said.

"Passion, when I say I am tired I really mean it. We have walked and walked and walked and walked. If I don't go out for a walk in a long time I will be fine with it."

Mitchell said, "Baby we really didn't walk that much. We went downtown and then to three malls. The time we spent in the malls total about 45 minutes. We knew what we wanted so it didn't take long. I think the problem was, the malls were all crowded. I mean no parking up front at all."

"At first I was cool with Mitchell parking on the back side of God's left hip and us walking together hand in hand to the mall entrance. However, after the second time I was done." We made sure not to laugh, as she rubbed her feet.

"Girl, you know I am not a mall lover any way, so I can't imagine going to three different ones. You all must have been in search of something really priceless." "Not exactly priceless, but something special," Samaria replied.

She and Mitchell pulled out a beautifully wrapped box. Whoever wrapped this gift, was anointed for gift wrapping. The paper was gold metallic and the ribbon was maroon satin, with a lily sticking out from the knot.

"Passion, Mitchell and I thought you and Kris would love this gift and we want you to wait for him to come home before you open it." I agreed, but of course you know I was probing for some hints, as to what the gift was.

They went to their room and changed their clothes. They were gonna come back down and eat with me. During the business of the day I managed to barbeque some chicken, cook some yellow rice and some seasoned green beans. The house reeked of good eating. We were going to sit down and then get down.

I changed into something a little more comfortable, when I am in the house I love my old Clark College warm-up pants and t-shirt. Talk about being able to relax and lay back with a good book. I don't even put on any shoes, just footies. Ahh, the good life behind closed doors. Of course when Kris is home, my attire will be a tad different.

After dinner I told Samaria and Mitchell to go on and relax and I would wrap things up in the kitchen. I rinse all of the dishes and place them in the dish washer. I put the leftovers in containers and then in the fridge. They will taste even better tomorrow.

I had already taken a nice hot bath, so I got ready for bed. I planned on reading a good book while waiting for Kris to call. I nestled into my pillow and the reading began. My book started to get really good and my cell phone rang. I quickly grabbed it and said, "Hi baby, I was waiting for your call." "I knew you would be. What are you doing?" I paused and realized that it wasn't Kris' voice, it was Terry.

"Why in the world are you calling me Terry?", I shouted.

"I am calling, because you keep avoiding me. I need to talk to you about us. You walked away without one word. How could you do that, and marry another man?"

"First, of all Terry we were not a real item and you know it. It seems to me it was okay, for you to walk out of my life when we were in college, but you have a problem with me moving forward. I made a change in my life and that change did not include you. Terry, you are no good for me."

"So, Passion are you saying you are better than I am?" "Terry, don't make this something that it isn't. You know good and well I have never been that kind of person. You were aware of the fact, that I gave my life to the Lord Jesus Christ and anyone or anything that was a distraction had to go. You had to go Terry."

"Listen, Passion I am not going away until we get together and close the chapter on our life because that has not been done. I am so hurt and you don't realize how it felt, to stand there and watch you give yourself to another man."

I started to yell, "Terry, you have lost your mind?" I had to calm down before I woke Samaria and Mitchell. "You certainly are not hurt, because you had another woman on your arm at my wedding that you were not invited to. So, if in fact you were hurt, it's your own fault and you deserve it. I have had it Terry and I want you to stop calling and harassing me or"…"Or what Passion, you're gonna tell your husband? I'd like to see you explain to him you were still seeing me when you were dating him. I don't think that will come off good at all. Either we meet and close our chapter or I will be the one telling your husband."

"Terry, you wouldn't." "Passion, I will and I you know I will. The choice is yours, meet with me *church girl*, or your little "*secret in the pew*" will be exposed."

I was in such shock. I couldn't believe he was playing the blackmail card. I had to do something, and that something was to meet with him like he wanted or my marriage might be on the line.

"Alright, Terry I will meet with you in the morning. The meeting place is my choice and we will only talk for thirty minutes, if the chapter can't be closed then don't show up.

Meet me at the Coffee Shop in Shannon Corners at 10:00am. The earlier the better, because I have a few things to get done before my husband comes home."

"Don't worry that is enough time and I will be there. I "pray" you don't change your mind and not show up because that would yield ugly results."

"I am hanging up now Terry and don't call back." He attempted to say something else, but I hung up. The phone rang right back and I answered with frustration in my voice. "What do you want?" "Whoa, whoa hey baby it's me. What's going on?" "Oh, Kris I am so sorry honey. Someone has been calling my cell phone and hanging up. They have called three times and it was starting to aggravate me. I didn't mean to yell at you."

"I know you didn't. If the phone rings again after I hang up, don't answer it. Aside from all of that phone drama, how was your day?"

"It was great honey, everything came on time and I have been working on getting a few more things organized around the house. I have enjoyed my quiet time though. How about you, how was your meeting?"

"The meeting was fine and it appears it's a done deal. The company likes what we presented and I will be heading their branding campaign. That includes a hefty bonus."

"Congratulations my love, you deserve it. I am so happy for you. You know the favor of God is upon you, not just favor but "uncommon favor". I am sure there is more to come." "Yes, there is more honey and guess what I will be coming home tomorrow afternoon, so we can finish up our honeymoon before I officially return to work on Monday."

Oh, no what am I going to do? Kris is coming home and I have to meet with Terry. I am going to be ruined. I was shaken from my wondering thoughts by Kris' voice.

"Honey, are you there? Did you hear me?" "Yes, yes I'm sorry there was delay in the phone I heard you, that is good news. What time does your flight come in?"

"I arrive at 12:30 and I will be coming straight home to my sweetheart. I so, want to be there with you watching a movie right now."

"That would be so nice, Kris. Curling up with you, would be better than curling up with a book. I am glad, that tomorrow night it will be a totally different story."

"Well, baby let's pray: *"Father in Jesus name, I want to say thank you. Thank you for protecting us throughout the day and I thank you in advance for covering us throughout the night. Please forgive us for any sins we have committed and teach us to forgive others that may offend us. Give me traveling mercies on my flight home tomorrow and allow me to be a witness to someone along the way. In Jesus name I pray, Amen."*

I love you honey. Rest well and I'll see you tomorrow, Lord willing." "Amen, thanks for calling honey and I'll see you tomorrow." We hung up; I put my book away and laid down with a lot on my mind. I am going to need God to help me through tomorrow.

CHAPTER TWENTY NINE

I woke up this morning with an awful headache and rightfully so, I have a lot going on. I got up and took my shower. It was 8:00 and I didn't want to get caught in traffic and because it's raining, people tend to act as if they can't drive.

While I was flat ironing my hair Samaria knocked on my bedroom door and while yawning said, "Morning, what's up? You sure are up early." I looked at her and smiled, "Kris is coming home today. He landed the branding deal for one of their clients, which yielded him a huge bonus and an early dismissal." She laughed.

"That's good God is moving for you all already. You know the word says; "A man that finds a wife, finds a good thing and obtains favor from the Lord." I got chills when she said that, even though I did say that in a round about way to Kris last night.

"What do you and Mitchell have going on today?" She sat down on my bed and said, "You know what nothing. We are going to hang around the house and go on line and to house hunt." "You guys are in the market? I thought you loved your house. Besides, Phoenix is beautiful."

"Yes, Phoenix is beautiful, but we are not looking in Phoenix, we are looking here." I dropped my flat iron and screamed, "You all are moving here?!!"

"Mitchell and I have been praying about it and we feel the Lord leading us here. We have had our issues but since Mitchell rededicated his life to the Lord, things have changed and we have been seeking God for direction in a few areas of our life. His past is forgiven, but he feels Phoenix has too many bad memories and he wants us to have a fresh start. So, we prayed about where we should move and the Lord said, Atlanta. As soon as we find a house, we are going to make an offer and if we can't sell our home since it's paid for we will let my brother and his family move in and give up that too small apartment."

"This is amazing, more family to hang out with. Kris is going to be excited to hear this news. He said to me while we were gone that he enjoyed you all being here. I'm sure he will welcome you all staying here until you find a house. What about your jobs?"

"Mitchell can transfer here and I can always find a new job. You know the recession stuff doesn't scare me. He will go home and work that out and I will stay here and job search."

I looked at my watch and it was 9:15. "Girl, I have to run I have an appointment at 10:00am. We will talk as soon as I get back. Yes, we are gonna be roomies."

I finished my hair and headed to the Coffee Shop, I wanted to get this meeting over. I was glad the closure was coming. This was long overdue.

I pulled into the parking lot of the Coffee Shop. It was 9:57 and I didn't see Terry's car. I was thinking maybe he had backed out and decided to stay with his date from the wedding. I was going to wait until 10:05 and then I was going to leave.

I looked at my watch and up again, as Terry walked out of the Coffee Shop over to my car. I got out before he could get to the window. I walked past him with an attitude and went in to the counter to order a caramel frappe.

Terry stood beside me and leaned on the counter. "Hey there beautiful, what's up? You look a little mad. You okay?" He said in a sarcastic manner.

I told the cashier, "Thank you", took my drink and sat down at a table. Terry followed me like a little puppy. "Okay, Terry what's up? Let's get on with the closer."

His sorry tail started laughing. "You act like you're in a hurry. You don't want to be seen with me or something?" As he makes the statement he reaches over to touch my hand. I snatched it back quickly. "You are afraid of my touch aren't you girl? You know I have what it takes to make you smile."

"Terry, I did not come here for your foolishness. We are now face to face, so talk." I looked at him directly for the first time since being there. When I did oh my goodness, I looked at that gorgeous smile with those pearly whites, he all of a sudden smelled good, and he was wearing a button down lavender shirt and the first three buttons were not buttoned. Of course the shirt looked like he got it from the cleaners' right before he met me. I was drawn back in when he started speaking.

"Passion, you know we had a good thing going. We didn't see one another all of the time, but when we did it was great."

"Terry, it was wrong and it was just to sleep together. You know that. I have moved on with my life, and this meeting is about to be cut short. I am not here to work out some sort of deal. I am happy with the man God has given me and I know my life is much better off."

"Girl, please no one will make you as happy as I have. I hear you though and you seem to be very serious about your relationship with "the Lord" and all. I can't help the fact that I still want you. You are really a good woman. You're fine, you're smart, you've got a great job and uh, you know."

"Terry, that's it we are done here, I have to go. I have other things to do and people to meet. You really need to figure your life out and call me once you've made some serious changes like given your life over to Christ so that I can rejoice with you. This chapter in both of our lives is now closed."

"Okay, okay I'm sorry. I'm done; I didn't mean to disrespect you. I will leave you alone. I have to admit I was crushed when you walked down that isle, because I knew I could have been the groom if I had only done right by you. I do wish you the best.

Friends?" He reached out to shake my hand. I looked at him for a moment and then extended my hand. We shook and it was a done deal.

"I have to go Terry, I have another appointment and I need run back home first." "Okay, I understand. May I please ask a favor of you?" I was leery of saying yes, but I did. "Yes, what's the favor?" "I had someone drop me off, can you please give me a ride home. You know I don't live far from here at all."

"Sure, Terry I can do that much for you."

We got in the car. I buckled my seat belt, backed out and headed to his house. It would normally take us about ten minutes, but with the rain it might take twenty.

I turned on a CD I had in the player, and relaxed as I thought about all of this being behind me. Terry hadn't said anything; he was just looking out of the window. I begin to wonder if he was really hurting. I had never seen him this way before. He used to be the guy that didn't worry about someone breaking it off with him, because he had women standing in line.

I turned down the main thoroughfare, that would lead to Terry's street. It was very curvy so I had to be careful.

As I started down the street, I looked at Terry and asked, "Are you okay?" He said, "I'm fine, just thinking." "You mind if I ask what about?" I replied. "No, I was thinking about what we had. You know, it did mean a lot to me." I assured Terry, that God had chosen the right woman for him. He just had to have patience.

He looked at me and frantically said, "Why can't it be you?" and reached over and touched my knee. I swerved, trying to knock his hand away. "Don't do that Terry", I said. "You know you like it." He replied and he reached up to my thigh. I screamed "No", hitting him again and let go of the wheel not realizing, a truck was coming toward us in the other lane. By the time I did realize it, it was too late. Everything went black.

CHAPTER THIRTY

I opened my eyes and I heard lots of voices and saw so many flashing lights. My head was pounding and I couldn't move. I looked over at Terry and he wasn't moving either. His eyes weren't even open and his hand was on my knee.

I tried to speak, but couldn't. I heard a man yell, "Hey, her eyes are open." A female came over to me and said "Mam, we are going to get you and your husband out of here. Just hang on try not to move. Your legs are trapped and we want to get you out safely."

The tears begin to roll down my cheeks, because I couldn't think of how I was going to explain to Kris what happened. I sat there and cried and prayed.

After a few minutes of some of the men working on releasing Terry, I over heard one of the paramedics say, "There's no pulse, he's gone." My face got hot and I went numb, I couldn't believe it Terry was dead. This has to be a bad dream; it isn't supposed to be this way. I was only taking him home. Everything went black.

When I woke up I was in the hospital. There were nurses and doctors in the room. I heard them, but couldn't make out what they were saying.

I begin to speak. "Hello, help me." "Mam, I am Nurse Diane Johnson, please try not to speak. I'm going to ask you a few questions and I only want you to blink your eyes. Two blinks for yes and one blink for no. Do you understand?" I blinked twice.

She began her questions. "Do you know where you are?" I blinked twice. "Good", she said. Are you aware of what happened?" I blinked twice again. "I am going to give you a pen and pad do you think you can write down an emergency contact number?" I blinked twice. "Great". She held the pad and I scribbled Kris' name and cell number on the pad. The nurse had a hard time, but she did her best to make it out and I blinked until she had every number right. She left to call Kris and another nurse took over until she came back.

I closed my eyes, hoping this was a dream and I cried because my legs were hurting so bad. Nurse Johnson came back in the room and said, "I reached Mr. Thompson. Is that your husband?" I blinked twice. "Who was the man in the car with you? Was he your brother?" I blinked once. "Was he a family member?" I blinked once again. "Was he a friend?" I blinked twice. "Okay, we found his cell phone hooked on his pants and someone is going to reach out to his mother. I'm sorry to tell you mam, that he didn't survive." I begin to cry really hard. She wiped my eyes with some Kleenex, and told me to try and calm down.

I heard my phone ring; my purse was in the chair next to my bed and I wanted to answer it so bad but I couldn't. One of the nurses answered the phone and came over to me. She asked if I knew someone named Samaria, I blinked twice. She then asked if she was a family member, I blinked twice again. I heard her say okay, we'll see you shortly. The nurse hung up the phone and told me that Samaria was on her way. She had gotten a call from my husband, who was headed to the hospital now from the airport.

This is what brings me here today, lying in this hospital bed looking out the window at the sun that was now coming out. As I mentioned, Pastor Gresham did say, "Be sure your sins will find you out."

This was going to be hard and I pray that I don't lose Kris. I closed my eyes, trying to erase what was happening. I heard someone say, "I am looking for Passion Thompson." The nurse replied, "Are you family? Then right this way." It was Samaria and Mitchell they beat Kris to the hospital. Samaria broke down crying, but quickly got herself together and begins to pray. Mitchell took me by my hand and said, "Kris is on his way Passion, hang in there."

At that time, they bagged Terry's body. When they held his head up Samaria saw it was him and looked at me with all sorts of questions in her eyes. She asked Mitchell to go downstairs and wait for Kris. He asked if she would be alright and she assured him she would. I wasn't sure I was going to be though.

"Passion, I know you are in pain right now. I have to ask you though, were you and Terry together." I blinked, yes. She hung her head in hurt. I wish I could explain. I tried to whisper. The nurse saw me trying to talk and told Samaria they didn't want me to.

The nurse turned and walked out and Samaria said, "Go ahead and try and tell me now." I whispered, "It's not what you think." She said, "Okay, but I want to know what it was." It truly hurt me to talk, but I had to say something. "I met him, to get him off my back and was taking him home when the accident happened." I started crying again. Samaria said, "Girl, please don't cry. We will get through this." As soon as we stopped talking, Kris came running into the room. He looked at me and begins to cry. Samaria got up and let him sit down. He took my hand.

"Baby, I love you. I am so sorry this happened to you. I am going to make sure you are well taken care of." I tried to speak, but Kris told me not to. There was so much hurt in his eyes and I knew I was the reason for it.

As Kris sat there holding my hand, the doctor walked in. He begin to talk to us, "Good afternoon, Mr. and Mrs. Thompson I am Dr. Lawrence Haygood and I am the doctor on duty today here in the emergency room. Do you all have a regular family physician?
"Kris answered the question and gave Dr. Haygood the information.

He continued, "It appears Mrs. Thompson, that both of your legs were penned when the telephone pole fell on top of your car. Your left leg was only scratched up and is swollen. However, your right leg is broken in three places and requires surgery. We've already drawn blood and taken your vitals. We will have to wait for the swelling to go down before we can do the surgery and that may take a few days. We have admitted you, started you on some pain medications and an IV. You will be moved to a room shortly and we promise we will take good care of you."

Kris had a few questions, but he didn't want to disturb me so he walked out into the hallway with the doctor to ask them. I felt so bad, because not only is my husband hurting because of my accident but he will also be hurting, when he finds out that Terry was in the car and why. As well as the financial strain this is bill is going to put on us.

Samaria came up to me and sat back down. "Okay, cousin we have to talk. I know it may be a little hard, but you have to tell me some things." I thought about what she was saying, but I knew within myself the only person I needed to talk to right now was Kris. I got the strength and just above a whisper said, "I have to talk to Kris first. It is going to be hard so, I need your prayers. Once I talk to him I will definitely talk to you."

"Okay, I understand and I certainly respect that."

Kris walked back into the room with a disturbed look on his face. I knew they must have told him about the deceased male passenger. "Honey, I know you are trying to rest, but the doctor told me about the accident. It appeared that you veered off the road and ran into a telephone pole. He also told me that there was a man in the passenger seat and he died. Baby, what's going on?"

I tried to sit up, but it was hard so I just put my head back down and begin to talk to Kris. "Honey, it is a long story but I am going to give you the abbreviated version. The man in the passenger seat was my old boyfriend from college. Right around the time you and I begin talking he showed back up and we went out and spent time together a few times. It wasn't a good for him to be back in my life, but it happened. Once you and I started dating, I walked away from him but I didn't close the door on that chapter of my life. Therefore, he showed up at the wedding, called me while we were on our honeymoon and last night he called and threatened to tell you about our past unless I agreed to meet him and officially close the chapter on our life." I paused to see if he wanted to say anything. He had his head bowed with his forehead resting in his hands and he looked up as if to say keep going and I did.

"Right before you called me last night he called. That's why I was so frustrated when I answered. He was trying to say that we weren't over and we still had a future together, but I wasn't agreeing with him. I should have however; completely broken it off and not tried to avoid   it. I didn't want to see him though, because I still had too many fleshly feelings for him. I didn't love him but I was addicted to him." I had to take a break from talking because I was winded. "When I met him this morning, I told him it was over. Leave me alone and go on with his life. He agreed and he apologized. He asked if I could please give him a lift to his house because he had someone drop him off. I only agreed because we had settled everything. On the way to his house though, he felt the urge to try and touch my leg, I pushed his hand away and he tried again. When I pushed his hand away the last time, I lost control of the steering wheel thus landing me here and he ended up dead. I didn't mean it Kris; I was trying to do what was right. I didn't mean for Terry to die or for us to be stuck with a huge medical bill. I'm sorry, I'm sorry, I'm sorry." I begin to sob uncontrollably. My entire body was shaking. Kris sat up and hugged me as best he could. In my ear he was whispering, "I love you Passion, don't worry about it. We will work through it. I just want you to get better baby." He sat there and held me. I felt so bad and my heart was breaking for Terry's family.

CHAPTER THIRTY ONE

Samaria was in the room when I talked to Kris. She and Mitchell stood off to the side and she was lying on his shoulder crying. They both looked so sad and hurt as well.

The atmosphere was so gloomy and I wanted this all to be a dream but it wasn't. There was a knock on the door, Samaria opened it. It was Terry's mother. She was crying and she was upset. I can only imagine, that she wanted an explanation. Why would the medical staff allow her to come into my room any way?

She came over to my bed. Kris stood up in a protective way; she reached out and shook his hand. She looked at me, "I am grateful that your life was spared, she said. I am hurt because I lost my only son. I have no idea what happened, but I don't believe it was intentional. Terry never got over you and just a few days ago I told him, he had to. He was convinced, that you all were going to get married and have children. He has pictures of you all over his bedroom and a photo album filled with your pictures from college. No one was aware, that Terry had a few mental issues and he was on medication. He was actually suicidal. Today my heart aches, but at the same time my load is lighter. He was a good child and he always meant well. Again, I don't know what happened, but at some point when you are better can we please talk?" I looked at her and nodded, "yes".

"I apologize for having taken up your time from your family, I must go but I will keep you in my prayers. Please pray for me and my family as we plan a funeral and heal from our loss. God bless you and get well soon." With so much pain she turned and walked away. Before she could reach the door, Samaria grabbed her and hugged her. She released a loud wail and we all begin to cry. Samaria begins to pray and I felt the atmosphere change. Terry's Mom grabs her stomach and says, "Help me Lord, Help me Lord." Samaria assures her that He will. She starts to calm down and Mitchell walks with Samaria as she continues to console her.

When they leave, Dr. Haygood comes back in to check on me and make sure I'm doing okay. He informs me that he will make sure the doctor coming on after him, will be brought up to speed on my condition. He tells us that I will need medicine for pain, inflammation and to prevent infection. He understands that I will be sore for a while but the meds should help me.

Mitchell came back while Dr. Haygood was talking. I didn't see Samaria and was wondering where she was. Dr. Haygood said he would be back before his shift ended and by then, he should have the test results (if there are any) from the blood that was drawn earlier. Kris told him thanks for all of his help and he left.

I asked Mitchell, "Where is Samaria?" He told us that she had gone down to the Chapel to pray. He asked Kris, "Are you hungry?" Kris stood up and stretched, "I could use a sandwich man. Let's walk down to the cafeteria. "Baby, try and get some rest while we are gone. It won't take us long and maybe Samaria will be back before us." Kris kissed me on my forehead and they walked out.

I turned over and closed my eyes. The scene from right before the accident kept playing over and over in my head. I couldn't stop it. I was so regretting not handling this sooner. Had I, none of this would have ever happened. I pray that God will forgive me and afford me the opportunity, to help someone else that may be found in my situation. I finally dozed off.

When I woke up, my parents, Kris' parents and the Pittman's where in the room. As soon as I opened my eyes, my Dad rushed over to the bed and said, "My baby, how are you feeling?" He had tears in his eyes. I still could hardly talk but I managed to say, "I'm okay Daddy and I'm going to be fine. One of my legs is broken in three places and as soon as the swelling goes down they are going to do surgery. How long have you all been here and are you all okay?" They all said, "Yes, we are fine, just concerned about you." They made me feel good. I pray they feel the same way, once they find out how the accident happened. I could tell Mom didn't like seeing me this way, but she came because she loves me. She eventually made her way over to hug and kiss me before they left.

They didn't stay that long; they wanted to get back home before it got too late. Mom and Dad don't believe in pulling all nighters. I almost made myself laugh thinking about that. That's where, I got not staying up late from.

Kris has yet to see that side. He will soon and that isn't because of the medicine they have me on either.

I don't know what happened, but they started talking among themselves and forgot about leaving. While the parents, Aunts and Uncles were chatting, in walks my brother, Kris, Mitchell and Samaria. Paul yells out, "What is this, a family reunion?" Everyone tried to laugh. He made his way to me and said, "What's up crip? I heard you stomped the devil so hard, that you broke your leg in three places. He ought to be afraid, be very afraid." I laughed but it hurt so I had to stop. "You are the silliest, but I love you." He kissed me on my cheek and whispered, "For real, I heard what happened. I'm praying for you." Paul, praying for me was something special.

My room was packed and I was over my limit on visitors. None of the nurses had come in to say anything, so we rode it out. I may have spoken to soon, there was a knock on the door, Kris answered, and it was Dr. Haygood. When he walked in he looked around, as if to say why are all of you in here? He didn't though. He beckoned for Kris to come over to my bed. When Dr. Haygood walked over, I noticed the flowers and balloons that had been sent over by my co-workers. The bouquet was beautiful.

All of a sudden I thought to ask Paul about Precious and the baby. He is going to stay with her and help her out. They get along well, so I know it's a good situation. "She's doing well and so is the baby. I swear it looks like she has grown since last night." I smiled. I could tell he liked being an uncle.

Paul walked back over to the rest of the family as Dr. Haygood talked to Kris and I. "I just wanted to come in and talk about the blood work that the lab sent back to us. I couldn't help but hear your brother talking about a baby. Did someone in your family just have one?" Kris said, "Yes my sister-in-law, just a few days ago." "You all must be pretty happy?" We nodded.

Dr. Haygood continued, "Well, after getting the blood work back, we are going to have to change your medication. You will still be treated for all of the things I mentioned earlier, however, because of the baby"....

"The baby?" everyone yelled.

"Yes, the baby. Mr. and Mrs. Thompson, congratulations, the blood work shows that you are pregnant. We are not sure how far along yet, but we will know soon. The pregnancy hormone can show up even if you are you just a few weeks." Kris looked at me, Samaria had her hand over her mouth, Mom put her face in her hands and Dr. Haygood knew it was time for him to go. He walked out of the room and everyone else followed

Kris, stood up with his hands in his pockets, and he looked at me and said, "Passion, you have some explaining to do and I know now is not the time to do it. Our family is out in the lobby, counting right now and we have to come up with something. Either we are good or you fell. We both know with the way things look, this baby has the potential of not being mine, but Terry's you're the only one that knows the truth. I love you baby and I'll cover you until this all blows over. Right now, I am going to ask for the test to be re-done. I'm praying that there was an error. I do love you and I do trust you and I am not going anywhere. We however, need to have a serious talk and work out some issues because I didn't sign up for this. "

"God, I have made a mess and I need your help. You know that the only man that could be the father of this baby is Kris. Please vindicate me and restore my husband's trust. I didn't mean for this to happen and I see how important it is for us to make sure, that we close the chapters in our lives as we walk into the new ones. I thank you for revealing the truth and for making things better for my Kris and I. I vow that this day will be the beginning of my new life with you, as I make sure I keep it clean with Kris and anyone else in my life. I love you Lord and I thank you in advance for making things right. In your son Jesus name I pray. Amen."

Samaria came into the room almost immediately after I prayed and said, "Passion, I was praying in the hall and I heard the Lord say, "He was making all things well and for you not to worry but watch Him work it out." Only you know what that means and I am in agreement. I also, heard Him say that all you are going through right now is the beginning of *"Passion's Progress" (No More Secrets)*. I smiled and drifted off to sleep.

To order copies of this book, the youth devotional
"From the Spirit to the Heart of the Young" or
schedule Evangelist Regina Howard for a speaking
engagement email our office at:
info@asoundvoicelive.com